Colin Blake and Rose Adams find themselves caught between their desire for each other, their fears, and their loyalties. Rose is devoted to her father, who will go to treacherous lengths to derail her affair. Colin fears his British operative job might endanger Rose's future. The two must navigate a path of heart-wrenching choices and trials that will ultimately reshape their destiny.

Loyalty and Love

ISBN: 978-1-4874-4032-9
Cover art by Martine Jardin

Published by eXtasy Books Inc.

Look for us online at:
www.eXtasybooks.com

Loyalty and Love

By

Luann Lewis

Dedication

To my husband and to Ann Anderson, who always supports me. Also, to Hannah and Bella, who listen to my never-ending plot twists.

Chapter One: It'll Be like a Vacation

Colin Blake was not a man who considered himself *handled.* But the condescending voice at the other end of the phone line belonged to Howard E. Cobb, Colin's *handler.* Cobb was letting Colin know that there had been a change of plans. MI6 wanted Colin to take on a quick New York job before returning to London. Blake groaned and argued, "I was ready to head back today. There's no such thing as a *quick* New York job."

"This one will be like a vacation." Even buried in the hum of the long-distance line, Cobb's voice sounded whiney.

Colin glanced across the room at his scowl in the mirror. Lifting his chin, he unconsciously took stock. He was a suave example of a confident 1960s jetsetter and fit the role of the consummate travel agent. Working for World Travel was the perfect cover. In some respects, a travel agent job would have been more thrilling than slogging back to London as a weary British undercover operative.

He shook his head, thinking about how much he was looking forward to that reclining airliner seat. Giving up that dream with a sigh, he said, "You're wheedling, Cobb. Why bother? I can't exactly refuse."

"Don't be so dismal, Colin. You certainly are not an easy man to work with."

"Not easy?" Colin's voice rose and he drew a long breath.

"Oh, don't be aggravated." Cobb tsked at him. "Listen to

me. You'll be spending time in a lovely cabin in the Adirondacks, and you'll be with General Joshua Adam's daughter. You're familiar with General Adams, right?"

"Of course."

"Well, his daughter is quite attractive—a socialite—and it'll only be for five days. Sweet and painless."

"Five days trapped in the middle of nowhere, doing nothing, with a woman I don't know and don't care to know." Colin shook his head even though Cobb couldn't see him. "Spoiled daughters and babysitting—not my cup of tea. Get someone else to do it."

"You're in New York, Colin, plus this matter needs to be handled with diplomacy. There have been credible threats against the general's life and now against his daughter's. She's going to need protection while he tours assets in Korea. If the wrong people got ahold of his daughter during that time . . . Well, you understand the implications. It's in the interests of both Britain and America to keep this girl safe."

Colin didn't answer.

"They'll bring a car around to your hotel and the girl will be ready at four AM. A map will be in the auto. Got it?" Cobb sounded falsely cheerful, and Colin scoffed. "Got it?" Cobb repeated.

"Yes."

"Oh, and, Colin."

"Yes?"

"You'll find everything you need in the cabin, but if you run into trouble and need backup, Alan Bradford will be staying about two miles southwest of you. You'll see his place marked on the map."

"Bradford? Then why isn't Bradford doing this job?"

"Bradford is not . . . um . . . shall we say, discreet when it comes to women. We need someone who can keep their head about them."

Colin sniffed. "That's ridiculous. Why should I get punished because I don't act like a schoolboy?"

"The difference in your maturity is reflected in your wages."

Colin snorted, then hung up the phone. Wages? Colin knew he did well, certainly better than Bradford, but if an agent couldn't keep his mind on his work, he shouldn't be an agent, no matter how little he was paid. He kicked off his shoes and tried to get some sleep before it was time to go collect the girl.

True to his word, Cobb's people had the car ready. It wasn't as luxurious as Colin had hoped. Colin had expected to get a '62 coupe or something fast and fun. After all, this *was* General Adams's daughter. But he got last year's model, a '61. Well, it was too late to argue with Cobb now.

Driving towards the outskirts of the city to the general's New York mansion, Colin thought about how this was just one of a few lavish homes the man owned in various upscale locations. From what Colin knew, the general had residences in Martha's Vineyard and DC as well as here, in New York. The man was certainly wealthy.

Although only drunks and milkmen seemed to populate the street at this hour, Colin stayed aware of everything around him. Little things caught his attention. A burned-out streetlight, a garbage can knocked on its side, a wandering cat—not stray, wearing a collar—small details filed away or discarded. Colin had once been told that he was *hyper-aware,* but noting little details had often kept Colin alive.

When he reached the palatial neighborhood, the general's house was the only one lit. He pulled into the circular driveway. Well-manicured bushes lined the pavement, and the lawn was lush and dark green under the lamp light. All seemed serene, no rustling in the bushes. He began to scan the area as he exited the car, but a petite figure emerged from the front door, tiny suitcase in hand. Colin assumed this must be Rose Adams. Sprinting up the walk, he chastised her for leaving the house before being certain of who was outside waiting. Rose looked up at him with wide eyes. She stammered out an apology and appeared so stricken that he toned down his annoyance.

"I'm trying to keep you safe, Miss Adams." Grabbing her suitcase, he led her toward the car.

"I understand," she said, following behind him. "It's just, I've only worked with the Secret Service before, and even that has been rare. They do things a little differently." She bit her lower lip, then stood by the passenger door hesitantly. Turning toward him, she asked, "Is it okay if I get in now?"

"Of course." He moved to the passenger side and opened the door for her.

The ride started off so silently that Colin thought she was pouting. However, a few glances to the side revealed that she was simply looking out the window. Now and then she gazed down into her lap, her hands clenched together. Colin got the feeling that she was as miserable as he was. Apparently, neither of them enjoyed being stuck in this situation. Like him, Rose probably didn't relish the idea of spending five days cooped up with a stranger.

Colin cleared his throat. He had to remedy this situation. "I think we got off on the wrong foot, Miss Adams. We weren't properly introduced." He gave her his most charming grin. He had a way with women and figured he would be able to put her at ease pretty quickly. "I'm Colin Blake."

"I'm Rose Adams." Her lips curved up, but the smile didn't reach her eyes.

"Yes." He nodded. "General Adams's daughter."

"That's me." She sighed. "General Adams's daughter." She turned away and looked out the window again.

Colin gave her another glance. Cobb had told him she was a socialite. Somehow, she lacked the worldly air he had come to associate with those types of women—that attitude of entitlement and snobbery. She *was* attractive, just as Cobb had said, but not in that plastic, made-up, sprayed-up sort of way. Her hair was a warm coffee color. The simple braid hanging over her left shoulder picked up glints from the streetlights, and her skin reflected the glow of the moon. She wouldn't be hard to look at for the next five days—if he allowed himself that indulgence.

On the other hand, that was exactly why Alan Bradford *wasn't* put on the job. Bradford let himself get carried away with women. Colin never did. First, Colin considered himself a consummate professional. Secondly, he saw women as human beings, not playthings. Colin wasn't sure Bradford looked at women quite that way. Bradford's reputation was such that the secretaries at the bureau grimaced or snickered when he walked past their desks.

As far as Rose Adams went, Colin remembered reading that Rose had stepped into the role of hostess for her father's affairs some years ago. Apparently, her mother had passed away after a short bout with cancer. The magazines covered the elegant dinners and cocktail parties Rose and the general hosted. Invitations were sought after by those with political aspirations as well as other social climbers. However, sitting here in the car, the girl seemed small and docile. It was hard to imagine her at the head of the general's table, entertaining Washington dignitaries.

Colin began to feel a little sorry about the way he had scolded Rose earlier and he tried to make conversation. "Have you been in the Adirondacks before?"

"A few times."

"This will be my first visit." But after that, the conversation fell off and he let her ride quietly with her thoughts.

Once they got into the mountains, it took a while to weave through the back roads of the forest, but Colin got them to the lone cabin that was slated to be their home for the next five days.

Chapter Two: Not Used to Having Fun

Colin pushed the door open and switched on the lights. Someone had dusted but hadn't done a very good job of it. Still, it appeared the place had been opened up, aired out, and set up for them. Colin walked through and did a cursory check before returning to the car and retrieving the bags. Rose followed him into the cabin.

"It's a little chilly, but I'll get a fire started." Colin grabbed a couple of logs from a stack by the side of the hearth. *Store-bought wood, not fresh cut.* He noted the string marks on the sides. There was a bag of kindling, too, with the price tag still attached.

Rose set her purse in a chair and eyed the room. "Maybe some tea"—she looked toward the kitchen—"or whatever might be in there?"

The two of them moved quietly as he got the fire going. He heard the sound of the kettle, then the clunk of the cabinet doors as she searched for drinks and mugs.

"Would you prefer tea, coffee, or hot chocolate?" She called out to him.

"Tea, thanks. I suppose they don't have lemon in there."

The refrigerator opened. "No, but there's milk . . . and it's in-date, surprisingly."

"They told me the place would be stocked."

The fire was beginning to blaze, and the room started to warm up. Rose came in with two steaming mugs.

Colin walked from window to window, testing the locks. "Make yourself comfortable. I'm going to have a look around."

Rose set the mugs on the coffee table, then perched on the couch. He glanced over at her with a nod, then went to check the bedrooms. Beds situated under the windows—bad idea. Simple nightstands, both empty. Nothing under the beds. He inventoried both bedrooms, making a quick note of everything in each, possible weapons and probable hazards.

When he was sure all was secure, he came out and climbed up into the small loft that was toward the back of the cabin. He crawled around, inspecting the area, then slid back down the ladder. Now, *that* was a safe area—no way to get to someone up there from outside.

"All appears to be in order." He dusted off his clothes. After a quick hand wash, he came and sat on the couch, leaving a comfortable space between himself and his charge. Hoping to put her more at ease, he relaxed and leaned back, but Rose continued to sit up straight at the edge of her seat, sipping her tea silently.

After a few minutes, Colin cleared his throat and leaned forward again. "Look, Rose, I know this is not the way you're used to spending your free time. You probably have a bunch of young friends that you go shopping with or maybe you'd be out at a club or a restaurant, but the department wants to keep you safe during your father's trip. This might not be the kind of week you'll find fun, and I'm truly sorry for that."

With a small shake of her head, Rose answered quietly, "I don't like shopping or clubs. And I don't have those kinds of friends." She glanced around the room. "It's actually quite nice here. I enjoy peace and quiet." Setting her mug down, she let out a long breath and finally leaned back. "I'm not used to having *fun*, Mr. Blake. I'm a general's daughter."

Caught off guard, he stared at her for a moment, then

asked, "Don't general's daughters have fun?" He fought a little smirk.

She gave a sniff, paused, and then said, "Fun is not held as a high value in our family." Giving Colin a pointed look, she asked, "How about you? Do *you* have a lot of fun as a . . . a . . . bodyguard . . . or whatever it is you are?"

Colin smiled and placed a finger on his chin. He tapped a few times. "Hmm. I think there are moments this job holds an element of fun, at least for me."

"That must be a wonderful way to live." She turned from him with a sigh, and Colin felt his throat tighten. Something in her eyes, a melancholy, touched him.

How could a woman who looked and lived like her be so sad? Dozens of men must be flocking around and fighting to brighten her life. In Colin's experience, beautiful women were the recipients of gifts, flattery, and attention. Those things seemed to bring women a great deal of pleasure. Still, if ever there was someone who wasn't experiencing a pleasurable life, it seemed to be the woman at the other end of this couch. Or maybe her displeasure was with *him* . . . perhaps she just didn't like *him*.

"I apologize that you're stuck here, Miss Adams. It doesn't appear that this week will hold *any* element of fun for you."

Rose looked back at him with raised eyebrows. Then she gave him a chagrined smile. "Oh, I've offended you, Mr. Blake." Her voice fell like a silk blanket soothing his nerves and her expression became gently stricken. "I'm sorry we've gotten off on the wrong foot. That certainly wasn't my intention." She reached over and put a soft hand on his knee.

"I'm not offended." He smiled. "Truly. I was simply worried that you were preparing yourself for a miserable five days with me."

"Oh, no." She pulled back but, with continuing warmth, said, "You seem quite charming, Mr. Blake. I'm sure we'll have a lovely time."

"You can call me Colin."

"And you can call me Rose."

Colin reached out a hand. Rose took it with a small shake and a nod.

"Now, Rose, there's a matter of sleeping arrangements. To be safest, I think you'll need to sleep in the loft. I'll stay down here on the couch."

She frowned. "Wouldn't you rather have a bed? And, as for me . . . well . . . " She glanced upward. "Is there anything to sleep on up there? That loft looks rather bare."

"I'll be fine on the sofa, and I'll put a mattress up in the loft." He shook his head. "Just being extra cautious. If anyone got wind of us being here, they'd expect you to be in the back bedroom. That's hardest to get to." He nodded in that direction. "With all the trees surrounding the windows. But we don't want you in *either* bedroom. The loft is the safest place, and you can pull the ladder up behind you once you're in for the night."

Rose nodded. "Okay."

"One more thing, if something should happen to me, there's back-up. An agent in a cabin two miles southwest. That direction." Colin pointed toward a corner of the cabin.

"How will I ever be able to find it?"

"Here, I'll show you on the map."

He unfolded the map, and they went over the route she'd have to take in order to reach Bradford and get to safety. Colin was impressed at how quickly she caught on and felt sure she'd be able to navigate the woods. He pressed a flashlight into her hand and told her she should sleep with it under her pillow—just in case.

"And what exactly do you think might happen to you?" Her voice quavered a little with the question.

"Nothing, it's just a precaution." He smiled down at her.

"But for right now, the sun's up and the day is beautiful. Would you like to explore the woods? Are you an outdoor girl? Perhaps a hike?"

Rose nodded. "Would that be okay—to go outside?"

"It's just as safe outside as it is in here. We're assuming the *bad guys*—whoever they are—don't know our location." He winked and gave her a comforting smile.

"Then let me change my clothes." She disappeared into the bedroom, then shortly reappeared wearing jeans, sneakers, and a flannel shirt. She slid on a thick sweater and was ready to go. Colin donned corduroys, a turtleneck, and a pullover. Once they were out the door, he locked it and tested it to ensure it held. Leaves crunched under their feet and the air smelled fresh and sweet as they climbed the incline behind the cabin.

"At least you'll be running downhill if you have to go to Bradford." Colin chuckled as he caught his breath, and Rose nodded. They turned and looked back at the cabin below.

"It's a lot steeper than it seemed at first glance." Rose shook her head, then shielded her eyes as she gazed around. "It's lovely out here."

"It is." Colin grabbed her hand. "Come on. Let's see if we can spy on some animals."

They wandered around the hillside, peeking from behind trees. They found deer munching on late fall grass. A few times, they caught sight of a stray rabbit, a busy squirrel, or the flash of a small chipmunk. Each time, Rose gasped, then raised her hand to her mouth to silence herself. "This is not something you see around the city," she whispered, "except the squirrels. You see plenty of squirrels."

By noon, the two of them were chilled and ravenous. Colin peered down at her. Her cheeks were flushed, and her eyes were bright. Maybe she was having fun after all.

Chapter Three: Somebody's Something

Colin was surprised at how much he was enjoying the hike, and as they wandered together, he felt an unfamiliar tug in his chest. Suddenly, he realized he had a deep desire to erase the sadness from Rose's eyes. Yes, over the next five days, as often as possible, he resolved he'd make her eyes shine as brightly as they were shining right now. Obviously, their stroll along the sunlit trail was lifting her spirits.

But as he digested that thought, he gave himself an invisible shake. *Don't worry about her eyes, buddy. Worry about her life. Stay professional, on task. She's just a charge, nothing more.* Pulling away from her slightly, he asked, "Shall we go back and have lunch?"

"Good idea. I can't believe how hungry I am."

They returned to the cabin, then foraged in the kitchen until they found canned soup and boxed biscuits. It wasn't long before they sat at the table with their feast spread in front of them and hot tea in their mugs. After lunch, they sprawled on the couch, putting their feet up on the coffee table and dozing as they listened to music on a tinny-sounding radio.

Dusk had set in, and the cabin was nearly dark by the time they had awakened from their naps. The autumn chill was descending upon them, so Colin started another fire and then brought a couple of blankets out. They sat in the glow of the blaze, wrapped in blankets, and quietly talked as sparks snapped on the hearth. Neither of them moved to turn on the lights.

It was unusual for Colin to do as much talking as he was doing this evening. Ordinarily, he was good at drawing other people out. On dates, he'd find out where the woman grew up, what she liked to do, where she went to school, and, of course, if she had pets. Women loved to talk about pets. But somehow, Rose had cultivated these same types of conversational tricks, probably from years of entertaining her father's friends. Colin found himself telling her about his childhood, university days, how much he loved to roam the Scottish moors, and even about the black cat he owned back in the old days before he had to travel so frequently. Colin hadn't thought about some of those memories in years. Sharing them suddenly made him feel vulnerable, almost unprofessional, considering the circumstances.

To make matters worse, he realized Rose had told him almost nothing about herself. He had done nearly all the talking while she had taken in every word, looking up at him with those huge dark eyes and nodding. She acted as if everything he said was fascinating. He needed to take control of this.

"Rose, I've been blathering all night. Tell me, what do *you* like to do when you're not being a general's daughter?"

"Me?" She leaned back on the couch and pulled her knees up, wrapping her arms around her legs. "I don't know. I guess I'm always the general's daughter. That's my whole life." She had that sad look again. "I'm never *not* that. I guess I'm going to be somebody's *something* for as long as I live."

"Somebody's something? Why?"

She turned to him. "Because that's what I *do*. That's what I was born to do . . . to be . . . somebody's something . . . a daughter, probably a wife to some prestigious politician someday, and eventually a mother"—she grimaced—"to groom some other person to be somebody's something." With a shake, she uncurled her legs and said, "How about a little dinner?" She stood up and snapped on a lamp.

Colin rose off the couch, too, the magic broken. "I'll give you a hand."

Dinner was uneventful, and both were ready to change into night clothes as soon as they finished washing the dishes. Rose disappeared into the bathroom for a while, then emerged, day clothes dangling over her arm. Her demure pajamas peeked out from under her robe, and fuzzy slippers wrapped around her feet.

Colin stood and walked toward her, grabbing his bag. "My turn." With a grin and nod, he slid by, then closed the door behind him. The scent of her soap wafted over him as he passed her. Now, that scent surrounded him as he leaned against the door. With closed eyes, he took a long breath and allowed himself a moment to imagine how it might feel to nuzzle her neck, move down to her shoulder, and then—but he cut it off when he felt himself stirring below the belt. *Unprofessional . . . even dangerous.* This was *exactly* why they didn't assign Alan Bradford to guard her. Bradford wouldn't be able to control himself. Bradford had a problem with women. Why was Colin sinking into this now?

It wasn't that Colin didn't enjoy a fine woman. He appreciated women a great deal. Some were good friends, some were like a classic artwork, and some took one's breath away, but that didn't mean he had to take every pretty thing home to bed. Besides, Rose was different. She wasn't the type one would have a little fling with. And Rose could certainly take your breath away, but she could also be a companion, a confidante. He could sense that. As a matter of fact, in his estimation, Rose was more than just a *usual* woman. One could fall in love with someone like Rose—really in love.

Colin shuddered at that thought, then moved quickly to the sink and ran cold water. Leaning down, he splashed his face with the icy stuff. *Cold water? How cliche.* Grimacing into the mirror, he flung chastisement at himself. He needed that cold water, and lots of it. By the time he emerged from the bathroom, Colin had scrubbed his entire body down in an icy shower and had regained his wits.

"Would you like some more tea?" Rose called from the kitchen.

"No, just some water will be fine." His mouth was feeling rather dry.

She brought him a glass, then said, "I suppose it would be a good time to hoist the mattress up there if you can." She raised her chin toward the loft.

"Oh, I can . . . I think." He smirked and handed the glass back to her. Fortunately, the back bedroom was fitted with two single beds. He pulled a mattress from one of them, juggled it onto his back, then carried it to the ladder. "I may need your help," he told Rose. She set down the glass and followed him. He got the mattress part way up the ladder. Then Rose steadied it while he climbed up, then pulled it the rest of the way. It took just about everything he had to yank it up, and he realized he was pretty awkward doing it—so much for the knight in shining armor.

"It's a bit dusty up here, Rose. I apologize that you're stuck with it." He peered down at her.

She shrugged. "Maybe I can clean it up tomorrow. A few sneezes won't kill me."

He nodded, then slid back down to her. "Shall I help you up?" He reached out a hand and gave a little bow.

With a slight smile, Rose took his hand and moved to the ladder. Then she let go of him and climbed gracefully. He tried not to watch but couldn't help himself, justifying it by thinking he needed to make sure he could catch her if she slipped. Colin stepped up a few rungs to pass a duvet to her, then slid back down and reminded her to pull the ladder up behind her. Finally, he lowered the lights and fluffed up a pillow on the couch. He lay down and pulled a blanket over himself. *Day one, down. Four more to go. This wouldn't be so bad after all. Maybe Cobb was right – like a vacation.* And he drifted off into a light sleep.

Chapter Four: Off Grid

A scratching woke him up. Maybe it was a mouse. No, not a mouse. He knew better. He was wide awake instantly. One didn't do this job only to confuse nocturnal animals with actual danger. Someone was at the window of the back bedroom. *Wham!* The sound reverberated through the cabin.

It wasn't scratching anymore. Somebody had burst in through the back window, and now the shooting began. After glancing up at the loft and raising his hand to signal Rose to stay put, Colin ducked behind the sofa. A black-clad figure with a rifle emerged from the back and then kicked the door of the front bedroom.

"Okay, Colin," the man called out. "Where is she?"

Colin stood up, hands raised. "Bradford?"

Alan Bradford peeled off his face mask. "Where is she, Colin?"

"So, you've gone over?" Colin shook his head. "How much did it take to turn you, Alan?"

"You don't understand, Colin. This is much bigger than you . . . or me. This is bigger than money. Where is she?"

"*What* is bigger?"

"The resurgence of the Ottoman-Communist Coalition, Colin. This is bigger than any money they could offer, but if money is what it takes to convince you, I'm sure we can give you enough to make it worth your while. Imagine, Colin, spending the rest of your days on some tropical beach, not having to do this work anymore. We can make that a reality for you."

"The Coalition? Don't you remember last year, when they set off a bomb in Drey's Department Store? They killed children, Alan. You want to be a part of *that*?"

"Collateral damage, Colin. Just like you're going to be if you don't cooperate.

"And the girl?"

"And the girl, too. I'm sorry for that, but that's how history is made. I always respected you, Colin, and I don't mean you any harm, but I need to know where she is." Bradford raised his gun. As he did that, Colin leaned forward and grabbed the bottom of the couch, flipping it backward and knocking Bradford's aim off.

Colin leaped across the toppled piece of furniture and jumped on Bradford. They tussled with his gun, and the sound of their breath sawed through the air. With a grunt, Bradford fought off Colin, but as he squeezed the trigger, his arm was averted, and the bullets discharged into Bradford's neck. Blood spurted across Colin's robe, neck, and chin, then dripped across the floor. Colin stood up and stepped away from Bradford's body. "Are you okay?" He called up to Rose.

She peered over the edge of the loft with wide eyes. "Y-yes."

"We've got to get out of here." Colin started towards the bathroom. "Get dressed." He washed up quickly, then threw his blood-spattered nightclothes into the garbage. After slipping into pants and a sweater, he came out, glad to see Rose buttoning up her flannel shirt. "Got your luggage?" She nodded. "Let's go."

They went out to the car and were on the highway in no time. He pulled off at the third exit down and got on the pay phone. Cobb had to be notified. This situation was going to reverberate down a whole channel of their department.

"I'm going off-grid, Cobb."

"Colin, there are other safe houses I can direct you to."

"No, if they got to Alan Bradford, they could have gotten to anyone. Bradford said it was bigger than him. He said it was bigger than both of us. I'm not taking any chances. We're going off-grid until you can get this thing sorted, Cobb. I'm not interested in being a sacrifice."

"Understandable. But how will I reach you, Colin?"

"You won't. I'll reach *you*. It's just four more days. Once I return the girl safely to her father, we can go after these people without endangering her." Colin could sense more than hear Cobb nod.

"Check in with me when you can, Colin."

"I will."

Colin and Rose drove silently, taking several meandering backroads until he found exactly what he was looking for. *Timberlands Motor Lodge*. It looked like nobody had stayed there in the last fifty years and the parking lot wound around the back of the building. Colin used backup passports to register them as Mr. and Mrs. Peter Smith, newlyweds, who wanted a room overlooking the forest where they could have some privacy. With a knowing wink, the old clerk dangled the key in front of Colin and reminded him to use the *Do Not Disturb* sign. Colin assured him that he'd be doing just that.

At last, Colin toted in their suitcases, and the two of them sat on the bed and exhaled.

"That was Bradford . . . our backup?" Rose looked at Colin.

"Yes." Colin returned her glance. "You were very calm. Nice job."

"I felt safe up there in the loft"—she shrugged—"but I was worried about you."

"I'm pretty good at taking care of myself." He grinned, reached over, and pushed a lock of hair out of her face. "You, on the other hand, are the precious charge that I am supposed to be looking after."

She turned away. "Yes, my father would never forgive you if anything happened to me."

"Rose." Colin touched her chin. Gently moving her face toward his, he said, "It's not just for your father." He locked his gaze into hers. "If anything happened to you, I wouldn't forgive myself." Her eyes glistened momentarily, and he thought she might cry. The impulse to kiss her was so overwhelming that he was afraid he might actually do it, but he held his breath and was able to sit still.

Her throat moved as she swallowed, then whispered, "You're a very kind man. I've only known you for a few hours." She glanced downward, then continued. "But even after this short a time, it's difficult to sit this close to you and not . . . " She blushed, then pulled away and stood up. Clearing her throat, she asked, "Is it safe to get some sleep now?"

He collected himself and stood. "Yes, I believe for now we're okay." They turned toward the bed. "It's a double," he said. "You can take it. I'll sleep in the chair."

"Don't be ridiculous. We're grown-ups. We can sleep in our clothes and put a pillow between us for propriety's sake."

Colin nodded. "If you're sure you'd feel comfortable that way."

They awkwardly bumped feet a few times but were able to drift off quickly, considering the excitement of the night.

Colin awakened with the pink rays of dawn trickling through a crack in the curtains. At some point during the night, Rose had curled up around the pillow that separated them, cradling it like a large stuffed animal. Then she had pushed up next to him. He could feel the warmth of her body, her knees against his thighs, and her head against his back. She was snuggled so close that the two of them took up little more than half the bed. A smile moved across his lips. If she pushed any closer, he'd be on the floor. This gave him a cozy feeling, like when his cat used to doze in his lap. The way she nestled against him brought that same serenity, only better. He took a long inhale and decided to enjoy the moment. Who knew when he'd get another like this?

Too soon, Rose began to stretch and yawn. Then, when she glanced at how much of his side she'd claimed, she suddenly withdrew and stammered out an apology.

Colin simply chuckled and let her know she'd kept him warm. Her blush was quite pretty, but he couldn't linger on that. They had errands to tend to.

They grabbed breakfast at a local hole-in-the-wall. Then Colin found an army surplus shop and loaded up the trunk with supplies. After that, it was back to the hotel. He threw their luggage in the backseat and put out the *Do Not Disturb* sign. Turning the car toward the forest, he began a slow ascent up a backwoods road not too far from the motor lodge.

They unloaded everything at a clearing. Then Colin led Rose through the trees until he found a well-hidden spot. "This is where we set up camp," he said, and he proceeded to pitch the tent he had bought. He made a campfire and set out a couple of rickety folding chairs.

"I'm going to drive the car back down to the lodge," he told Rose. "I want it to look like we're still there in case we get visitors we don't want. Then I'll hike back up here." He handed her a pistol. "You know how to shoot, right?"

She nodded. "Of course. I'm a general's daughter."

"That's just in case you need it." He looked at the sky. "I shouldn't be long. It won't even be close to dark before I'm back."

CHAPTER FIVE: A MAN WHO'S NOTICED

Colin was wrong about that. It was nearly dusk by the time he returned, but Rose was calmly wrapped in a blanket and sitting by the fire when he crunched through the leaves and came up to the campsite.

"You should have had that gun raised. You had to have heard me coming."

Rose smiled. "I knew it was you."

"How?"

"You sometimes walk by stepping on the ball of your foot before your heel. That's not like other people."

His eyebrows rose. "Clever. I didn't notice that about myself."

"You're a different sort of person, Colin." Rose looked up at him without a smile, and he felt heat rise in his cheeks. "Not in a bad way," she added.

"That's a relief. I'm not really used to being noticed." He came and sat down on the chair next to her.

"Surely, that's not true. You seem like a man who is very used to being noticed . . . especially by women." With a tilt of her head, she made her skepticism clear.

"Not in the way *you're* noticing, Rose."

"Touché." She turned to face the fire. "So, why are we out here?"

"They'll find the motel at some point, and I don't want to be there when they do."

Rose nodded.

"I don't think they'll be able to find us out here, though. At least not before the time I'm supposed to get you home."

"And once I'm home?"

"There'll be no point for them to take you. Your father will be back. He won't have access to overseas weapons or plans at that point. Once you're safe with him, I can go after these people." He leaned back in the chair.

"And then?"

"Then?" He sighed. "Then I'm on to the next assignment . . . but before that, maybe I can ask you out to dinner . . . if you'd care to go."

Rose looked up at him. "On a date?"

"Do people our age date?" he asked.

"How old are you?"

"Thirty-five."

She shook her head with a tiny smirk. "I suppose not at *your* age, but I'm only twenty-six, so I still date." The campfire flickered across her face.

"Then a date." He grinned and nodded his head in a mock bow.

"My father won't like it, but I'll go . . . at least once."

Colin sat up straighter. "Why wouldn't your father like it? I'm an educated man with a good job. Fathers approve of me. Fathers love me."

"No, he won't like it." She shook her head. "He won't like you taking me out."

"I'll bring him around. I'm known as a good prospect . . . isn't that what it's called—a good prospect?"

Rose eyed Colin. "For some other girls, maybe, but not for *my* father. Still, I'd like that dinner with you. It would be different for me."

"You make me feel like a sixteen-year-old boy, Rose."

She gave a small laugh. "How is *that,* Colin? You are certainly the most sophisticated and charming man I've ever met."

Colin felt himself blush. "Well, I feel very awkward and off-kilter at the moment . . . asking you on a date, like a teenager."

Rose scoffed. "You probably didn't even have to ask girls for dates when you *were* a teenager."

"No, I didn't . . . because I was too scared. I wasn't at all good with women . . . with girls."

"I guess you've caught on since then."

"I wouldn't bet on it." He shook his head. "You'll find out when we go on that date."

They both chuckled.

Colin leaned back in his chair. She was right to some extent. He *didn't* have problems with women. He often found himself the pursued rather than the pursuer. That made it easy for him to have company whenever he desired, but Colin was more of a loner. He enjoyed solitude. When he went out with a woman, he often felt on edge, as if he had to perform—to be winsome and attentive. He ensured the wine glass was full, hung on every word, opened every door, held the chair, and helped the woman in and out of the car. He knew the right things to say and do, but it could get exhausting.

Sure, there was some of that behavior now with Rose. Colin certainly wanted to charm her, and of course, he prioritized courtesy, but because she was so serene, every smile he drew from her felt like a reward. And most of the time, in their conversations, she ended up relaxing *him* instead of the other way around. He'd find himself chattering on about something. Then he'd end up hoping he wasn't boring her to death. Still, with her nods and answers, he got the feeling she was truly interested in him.

After they finished their light camp dinner, evening descended over the forest, and it was easy to talk in the dark with just the fire lighting the night. They pulled their chairs closer together and stared into the flames as they spoke, blankets wrapped around them to keep out the chill.

"How did you learn to shoot, Rose? Are you good at it?" He glanced at her. Her skin shone with a golden hue in the flickering campfire.

"My father taught me, and I've been in hunting parties." She shook her head. "I have a notoriously bad aim when shooting at innocent beasts." Rose shrugged. "And I detest hunting altogether, but I suppose it's a social necessity." She pulled at some threads on the blanket. "I'm good at skeet shooting, though. I'm great when the gun is not pointed at a trembling animal."

He chuckled. "We'll have to compete some time. I'm not an avid hunter, but I'll bring down a pheasant if I intend to make a dinner of it. My aim is pretty true."

"I've brought down a pheasant or two. I can even prepare them—from forest to table." She shuddered. "But I'd rather do fish. Somehow, that doesn't bother me as much. Still, one does what they have to."

Colin chuckled. "I can't imagine anyone being *forced* to kill and prepare pheasant these days."

She looked up at him. "You'd be surprised what's expected of a person in my position . . . or at least the skills my father believes I should possess."

"For instance?"

"I can swim, scuba, sail, ski, speak three languages, play piano, play guitar, shoot, prepare an assortment of gourmet meals, go toe to toe with a sommelier, arrange flowers, sew, quilt, knit, crochet, sing . . . and I was forced to model for a charitable fashion event last year, it was featured in a Sunday magazine, so I guess I've got that under my belt, too."

Colin let out a long whistle. "Quite an impressive resume."

"That's exactly what it is—a resume."

"A resume for what?"

"For being a wife . . . to somebody."

Colin shook his head. "Well, what do you *like* to do? Any of that?"

"I like to read. And what I would like to do most in the world . . ."

"Yes?"

"Most in the world, I'd like to just sit and watch television, some show that would make me laugh, or maybe an adventure, and eat chocolates. I'd like to waste time and do something decadent." She looked over at him. "But I don't dare."

"You're twenty-six. I would imagine you could live your life any way you want to. You're an adult." He made his voice gentle.

She shook her head. "That would destroy my father. I'm all he has, and he has invested everything in me." She turned her face back toward the fire, her eyes glistening. A brief flash of the old fairy tale *Rapunzel* ran through Colin's head. Rose reminded him of the beautiful princess who was trapped in the tower. Didn't the prince climb up her long hair and free her . . . or was that just to visit her? How did that whole thing end, anyway? He couldn't remember. He vaguely recalled something about the prince falling into a bramble bush and being blinded. Giving himself a shake, he reached over and poked the fire with a stick.

Chapter Six: Something Much More

Rose Adams hadn't expected a man like Colin Blake to show up at her house the day before yesterday. Sure, she'd had experience with the Secret Service before. She was accustomed to those square-jawed, conventionally handsome men. They were usually former military, pleasant enough, but often quite stiff. Colin had the masculine jawline, but his curved chin was sort of cute and, well, kissable. She blushed at the thought.

It wasn't like her to notice those kinds of things. Still, Colin was remarkably handsome. Those blue eyes could make a woman's heart flutter. He'd grabbed her attention even when they first met and he was scowling at her, chastising her for coming out of her house when she shouldn't have.

She stole a glance at him in the firelight. The shadow of his lashes spread across the tops of his cheeks and emphasized the planes of his face and his long neck looked sleek and tan with the flames flickering across his skin. Lifting her shoulders, she squirmed in her seat, then shifted her focus to the fire.

Just staring at him stirred up all sorts of unfamiliar feelings. She had been on dates with plenty of men—good-looking men—but they hadn't had *this* effect on her, or any effect really. This reaction was new to her, and she wasn't sure she liked it. *Well* – she dug her toe into the sand as she considered the feeling—maybe she *did* like it. It was an exciting physical sensation. It was . . . it was . . . desire. She *desired* him. She wanted to press her lips against him, to taste the light sweat on his face and neck. *Scandalous thoughts!* And he had asked her to dinner. Did he desire her, too? She stole another glance at him.

Of course, there wasn't much she could do about it if he *did* desire her. Her father would never let this relationship go anywhere. She sighed.

"Tired?" Colin asked her.

Rose nodded. "A little. The outdoor air does it." She was glad he couldn't see her blush in the dark. She shifted again and took a deep breath. These feelings were unpleasant and delightful both at the same time.

"You can go into the tent whenever you want. I'll follow behind after I set some things up and take care of the fire. Pick whichever sleeping bag you want. I'll take the other."

She slid her shoes off outside the tent, and in a few minutes, she had both sleeping bags rolled out. She crawled into one of them. With the extra blanket over her, she was cozy. The night calls of the animals were like a lullaby. She tried to stay awake and wait for Colin, but her eyes closed against her will, and she was sound asleep before he came in.

Colin set up a tripwire around the campsite. He wasn't taking any chances. The night air got to *him,* too, and he was sure he'd be sleeping heavily before too long. The pans hanging on this wire would wake him if anyone came wandering close. Still, he figured it would be at least a day before whoever was after them got to the motor lodge and possibly another day before they found this little clearing. By then, he would have moved them to yet another spot. After that, he'd have her home safely. At least, that was the plan.

Once he got Rose back to safety, there was going to be clean-up to do. He and Cobb would have to work closely with the Americans to find out exactly how far the arm of the Coalition reached. It wasn't just in Europe at this point. That was clear. Obviously, they had penetrated the United States and probably Canada as well.

Colin poked the fire and spread the lingering embers, watching the small flare-ups pale. Had he caught Rose eyeing him earlier? Did she mistrust him? Had he made her nervous somehow? Maybe she regretted agreeing to the dinner date. Perhaps he should give her a chance to change her mind gracefully. Asking her to dinner had been terribly unprofessional. He should have waited until this thing was over. Colin's face burned. This was humiliating. How had he lost sight of himself that way? He didn't even really know the girl and he was acting like this. If he had any sense, he'd run for the hills. He shouldn't be around anyone who made him lose self-control this way. Now, he didn't even want to go in the tent. What if she felt awkward sleeping near him?

But exhaustion was overwhelming. As quietly as he could, he lowered the zipper of the tent door and crept in. He was relieved to see she was sound asleep. He slipped into his sleeping bag and was out within minutes. And when the birds awakened him in the morning, he lay there dozing to their cacophony of joy at the same time as he realized she had somehow managed to toss and turn during the night until her sleeping bag was pushed up against his, body snuggled close, her head on his shoulder and her knees leaning on his.

When she began to shift, he peered down at her and smiled. "I swear," he assured her, "I did not pull you over here."

He was rewarded with a return smile. "It's your magnetism." Her voice was husky with sleep, and she snuggled even closer. "I feel safer when I'm near you."

It seemed only natural to stretch out his arm. She lifted herself slightly, then rested in the crook of his shoulder. He pulled her snug. "You *are* safe. I'll keep you sheltered right here."

"This is good service, Mr. Blake."

"Only for the most special clients, Miss Adams."

"So, what are we going to do today?"

"I'm going to check on our motor lodge . . . to see if all is well there. Then I thought we might have a hike."

"That sounds fun."

"But first breakfast."

He didn't want to get up, though. He wanted to lie here, with her in his arms, at least until noon. But the scent of her hair was drifting up to him and was too enticing. He tilted his head down slightly to breathe it in. A few strands tickled his lips, and he knew if he didn't get away, he would soon be kissing her and burying his face in that cool silkiness. He wasn't sure he could stop with just her hair if he did that. Sensations traveled through him, along with visions of what it would be like to ravage her right now and hear her moans.

Colin suddenly pushed her away and sat up. "Let's get breakfast." He shifted himself, then turned and stood. "I'll start the fire and make us some eggs." With that, he headed quickly out of the tent. He could feel Rose's eyes on him as he left, but he couldn't face her. He didn't want her to see how visibly excited he was.

Of course, a man like Colin Blake wouldn't want a woman to be forward the way she had been this morning. Rose bit her lip as Colin left the tent. And how had she managed to get so close to him last night? She didn't remember moving around in her sleep, but she must have, just like at the hotel. What must he think of her? He was probably sorry now that he had even asked her out to dinner. She ought to offer him a graceful way to get out of it. Tears stung her eyes. He'd run out of the tent this morning as if he hated her. It was so abrupt. How humiliating. This was just a job to him. She had to remember that.

Rose pulled herself out of her sleeping bag and straightened her rumpled clothes. And she was such a mess. Maybe she even smelled. After all, she'd slept in her clothes last night. She reached for her hair and patted it. Oh, her hair was terrible, too, and she didn't even have a mirror. Rose tried combing it with her fingers, then pulled it into a messy braid. She had never been so mortified in her life. Generally, poise came easily to her, almost to the point of boredom. Of course, that was because she didn't much care what anybody thought of her. It was her father who cared. But she didn't want to be embarrassed in front of *this* man, not in front of Colin Blake.

But why not? After all, he's just a bodyguard. She reminded herself of that a few more times. Then, with a long breath, she emerged from the tent. By then, the fire was going, and eggs were beginning to sizzle. Colin also had a pot of water simmering.

He looked up and asked, "Tea or coffee?"

"Coffee." Her resolve melted. No, he wasn't just a bodyguard. He was something much more than that, and she wanted to be something more than a client to him.

Chapter Seven: An Unfortunate Problem

"So, what have you got planned for us today, Mr. Blake?" Rose leaned back in her chair, the eggs settling in her stomach. "After that great breakfast, I'm almost ready for a nap." She rolled her eyes. "But what I could really use is a shower."

"This isn't a campground, Rose. No amenities here." He grinned over at her. "I thought you figured that out when I sent you into the trees with a roll of tissue last night."

She grimaced. "Yes, I got the idea. Any lakes around?"

"There might be, but they'd be awfully cold."

"I don't suppose we could go back to the motor lodge just for a quick wash up."

"I'll find you a lake."

Shortly thereafter, Rose was following him up a trail. *I must be crazy. This is sweater weather and I'm gonna go diving into a lake.* But she couldn't stand being so grimy, especially in front of *him*.

They hiked around a bend and came upon a lake as clear as glass. The clouds and sky were reflected so beautifully that it almost seemed like the world had turned upside down.

"Are you sure you want to do this?" He looked toward her, eyebrows raised.

They had grabbed towels and a change of clothes from the tent. Now, she wondered if this was foolhardy. The water was gorgeous, but she was sure it would be cold. "Absolutely." The tremor in her voice betrayed her misgivings.

Colin chuckled and turned away. "I won't look. I promise."

Rose walked over to a flat rock and placed her things on it. She slowly stripped down, peeking over her shoulder to make sure he kept his word. It was chilly enough in the morning air that just standing there gave her goosebumps. She tiptoed down to the water's edge and stuck her toe in with a gasp. "Oh my." She took a huge breath, closed her eyes, forced herself to run a few steps forward, and then fell into the water with a scream. The cold shocked her system but filled her with a certain elation. She came to the surface laughing and daring Colin to join her.

"Close your eyes." He padded over to the rock and laid his things down. "No peeking." Colin began to unbutton his shirt.

Rose squinted and watched for a minute, then made herself turn away. The cold water brought her body to life. She had heard stories of people using cold showers to dampen their sexual excitement, but this lake seemed to be doing just the opposite. Maybe it was the fact that she was out here swimming in the nude, with nothing between her skin and nature. Whatever it was, she felt as if every nerve ending was alert and alive. All she could think about was how it might feel to wrap herself around Colin's naked body. He was a man of the world—experienced, debonair—surely, he would know how to make love to a woman. She had never done anything close to that. She had done nothing more than give a chaste kiss to a date who dropped her home after dinner and a movie. Her father would be appalled if he suspected she even thought about such things.

She heard Colin's yelp as he splashed his way toward her. "Can I turn around now? Are you decent?" she called.

"No, I'm not decent." He laughed. "But you can turn

around." His naked shoulders and arms still held a golden tone left over from summer, and he paddled toward her in the sunlight. "Don't worry, I won't come too close."

With a laugh, she assured him she wasn't a bit worried. "I can probably swim faster than you."

"Is that a challenge?" His eyes narrowed.

Rose nodded, then moved her body forward. "To that log over there." She jutted her chin. "On your mark, get set, go." The words tumbled out before Colin could even position himself, and she took off like a flash.

"Hey!" he yelled but was behind her in seconds.

Both of them pulled at the water with sleek strokes, Rose slightly ahead due to the quick start. Colin began to gain on her and was catching up. She increased her pace, fighting to keep her lead, but she could hear the pound of his paddling and sensed him close to her side. They reached the log at the same time and turned to claim victory. As they laughed, their bodies bumped. She allowed her front to linger against his for a moment, but he pulled back quickly.

Colin blushed and stammered. "I . . . I'm sorry."

"No . . . no . . . don't worry. I'm fine." She smiled up at him and moved a little closer. "That felt good."

But Colin put his arm out and pushed against her shoulder. "If you do that, I'm going to have trouble." He took a breath. "I'm going to have trouble controlling myself."

She slipped by him and was up against his body again. The feel of his hardness was a pleasant shock. So *that* was how men felt. Curiosity overtook her, but before she could do anything about it, Colin used both hands to push her away.

"No, not like this."

Rose realized she had been staring down into the water at his body. Now, she looked up into his face. "What do you mean, Colin?"

"I'm on the job. It isn't professional. I'd be taking advantage of you." He shook his head. "It would be wrong."

She briefly wondered if what she felt right now was the same as what men felt when they desired a woman. Rose had the feeling she was experiencing lust. There were reactions sparking all over her body that seemed impossible to deny, but it appeared Colin was having none of it. She continued to stare into his face as she tried to sort out her feelings.

"I don't want you like this," he told her. "I want to do this relationship right. I want to . . . to . . . *court* you. I want to take you out and do it the way your father would want."

"My father?" She saw her father's face in her head. That certainly helped tame her spirit. "Oh, my father." Rose stopped pushing against Colin's arms. She hadn't realized she was even doing that until her body relaxed and Colin lowered his hands. She blushed. "I'm a little embarrassed. It's just that things have been so crazy the last few days." She shook her head. "I keep thinking, what if I die? What if these people kidnap me? I don't want to go to my grave having never been with a man." Rose treaded water, turning slightly away from Colin. She knew that wasn't the entire truth. The man she wanted to be with *was* Colin, not just any man—but she supposed he would remain a dream.

Her father—nothing more needed to be said. Just *her father*. She would never have Colin because her father would never allow it. "I'll finish washing up," she told him. "It's frigid in this lake."

"Rose." Colin grabbed her arm and turned her back towards him. "You're not going to die. I'm not going to let that happen."

She looked into his eyes. They were even more blue with the lake reflected in them. She was sure he meant what he was saying. He intended to keep her alive, no matter the cost.

"Rose, you'll have many experiences of all types during

your long life." He smiled down at her. She wanted to cry, she wanted to hug him, she wanted to surrender her entire being to him, but all she did was just nod and remind herself that she'd probably never even see him after these five days were over. Her father had other plans for her.

Colin didn't mean to peek when Rose got out of the water, but he thought he heard rustling in the bushes, so he glanced just momentarily in that direction and caught sight of her perfectly curved waist and rear as she walked to the flat rock. He turned away quickly but couldn't erase the glimpse of her breasts in profile. Suddenly, he was contending with a mutiny from down below. That was a problem this morning. Between Rose extending an invitation and him allowing stray thoughts into his head, it was getting difficult to keep his raging hormones and their effects in check. Certainly, it would be difficult to fight the *bad guys* if he was wielding a jousting lance below his belt. He grimaced at the thought. He needed to keep his mind *and* his body on task.

Plus, he wanted to do this relationship thing right with Rose. He looked forward to meeting her father. He didn't believe for one minute that there would be a problem with the old guy. Fathers loved him. He wanted to take her out, bring her flowers, buy her gifts, and then, well, he'd see where it went from there. It wasn't impossible to see himself celebrating Christmas with her and New Year's Eve for sure. He imagined the two of them dancing together and kissing at the stroke of midnight.

"Are you coming, Colin?" She broke into his thoughts as she stood at the edge of the lake, fully dressed and toweling her hair.

"You have to turn away."

"Why?" she teased.

He tried to shrug and tread at the same time. "Okay, suit yourself." He headed toward shore.

"Oh my." Rose quickly turned her back. "You're not one to back down from a dare, I guess."

Colin stepped out of the lake and strolled to the rock. "I only have my dignity to lose." He picked up a towel and began to dry himself.

"Somehow, I don't think you'd lose that, even in the buff."

Once he was dressed, they headed back to their campsite.

"Feeling better now?" he asked her.

Rose nodded, but he sensed there was something she wasn't telling him. Perhaps he should have let her bathe alone. He shouldn't have come into the water with her. That was too forward of him. He bit his lip. It had been terribly ungentlemanly of him just to assume she would allow him, in all his nakedness, to swim in the lake with her. And they had actually touched bodies.

Colin felt like a fool. At the same time, the thought of her body gliding up to his brought an awakening to his groin as they walked. He lowered his arm so that the towel covered the evidence of his excitement and let Rose move slightly to the front. If she noticed him bulging, she would certainly be disgusted. Colin tried to get his thoughts into the right place. *Think about Cobb. Think about the eggs you cooked this morning. Think about Bradford.* That helped, and he believed his weakness at least wasn't visible any longer.

How would he ever be able to date this woman if he couldn't keep himself under control just walking in the woods with her? When they got onto a dance floor, would he embarrass himself this way, with a protrusion in his pants every time her body was near him? He shook his head and fought the feelings while at the same time noticing how smooth Rose's steps were as she moved down the path ahead of him. It was difficult to stop watching the sway of her hips and the way the tendrils of her hair floated around the thick braid.

Every bit of her caught his attention and didn't let go.

Chapter Eight: Donuts

Colin needed to get down to the motor lodge and check on things. Plus, he thought giving Cobb a quick call would be a good idea, but Rose insisted he go for a hike. He got her to compromise by allowing her to accompany him to the car and then ride with him to the pay phone.

Everything seemed quiet at the motor lodge. He stopped in at the desk and the old man was friendly, joking with him about the couple never leaving their room. That was exactly what Colin wanted. Let anybody who came by believe the two of them were in there. When he got back to the car, he switched on some music. They both enjoyed the temperate breeze and the nice melodies on their drive.

The bright sunlight took the edge off the early fall chill.

Colin caught sight of a bakery and pulled over. "Donuts?"

Rose nodded. "Sure. That's a treat I rarely get."

He came back with a half-dozen, having picked out some very decadent-looking chocolate ones. Rose sat in the car, nibbling at dripping frosting, as Colin went to a pay phone and made an overseas collect call to Cobb's office.

"You caught me just as I was about to leave, Colin, but I'm glad you called."

"No further news at this end, Cobb. We're still off-grid."

"I've been doing a little investigating, but I haven't been able to identify any other members—at least in Britain. It's got to be the Americans."

"Keep trying."

"Where can I reach you?"

Colin gave him the name of the motor lodge. "Just leave a message saying to call my father. I'll know who it is."

"Will do. Only three more days, Colin."

Colin was all too aware of that.

"We're working on expediting the tour, though. The general may be returning earlier."

Colin swallowed. "That would be helpful." Colin bit back an unprofessional stab of disappointment. But he reminded himself that the sooner this was over, the sooner he could start seeing Rose in a personal way.

They said their goodbyes, and Colin returned to the car. He gave Rose a long look. "You're a beast with that donut." Chocolate had stuck to her lips and smudged her cheek. He reached out a finger and dragged it across her face, catching the excess frosting. Then he held his finger in front of her. Suddenly, she leaned forward and sucked the chocolate off of it. He gave a little gasp at the pleasure that ran through his body.

Rose blushed and pulled away. "Well, you said I was a beast." Her chuckle betrayed her embarrassment.

"So I did." He raised the finger to his own mouth and slowly licked the last traces of chocolate off while meeting her eyes. "Perhaps I'm also a beast." He attempted to remain cool, but the usual battle with his excitement was raging.

Rose stared at him, batted her eyes a few times, and took a deep breath. Then she went back to her donut. "Mr. Blake, you really know how to live," she said between bites.

He reached into the bag and chose a sugar-covered pastry. Leaning back against the seat, he began to munch on it. "I enjoy the finer things." He closed his eyes as he chewed. "And when I enjoy them, I *really* enjoy them." Opening his eyes, he turned towards her and continued. "And I like for the people I'm with to enjoy the finer things, too."

She met his eyes. "I'll bet you do." He watched her tongue

explore the edges of her donut and let out a long sigh.

"I think we need that hike." He sat up, put his donut to the side, then started the car, pointing it back toward the motor lodge. She was finished with her treat by the time they got there. He grabbed the bag, and they hiked back up to the campsite.

"Let's go the other way on that fork we found yesterday." Rose pulled on his arm. Colin stashed the donut bag, grabbed their canteens, and shoved the rest of his donut between his lips.

"Wait," he said, garbled from a mouth full of pastry.

She laughed at him. "And you said I was a beast."

"You didn't give me a moment," he chided, barely understandable. "That's so unfair."

"Don't talk with your mouth full." Her smile broadened as he turned away. It was hard for him to believe this was the same woman he had picked up from that big house two days ago. She'd had no sparkle then, no smiles. Now, she was laughing and full of fun. This is how she should always be, he thought. This is how he wanted to make her life. And his insides suddenly felt as if he was *full* of donuts—soft and sweet.

Oh, this wouldn't do. He gave himself a shake and swallowed, but he couldn't get rid of the feeling when he looked at her. He wanted to touch her and hold her and . . .

"Come on, slowpoke," she called back to him, then reached and grabbed his hand. He caught up with her pace, and they hiked up the trail until it turned. They stopped abruptly at the sight of two moose in a small clearing. "Oh, Colin," Rose whispered. "Don't move."

They stood still. Then he led her into the bushes where they could watch, unseen, from a closer spot. The animals were glorious, huge with proud antlers and shiny pelts. Rose squeezed his hand, her excitement contagious. Finally, she looked up at him, eyes glowing. "This is amazing."

"It is." He smiled back. Then his smile turned to a grin. "You've got leaves in your hair. It must have happened crawling through the brush." He gently pulled them out. Her face was tipped up, and the feel of her breath on his skin was too much for him. Before he realized what he was doing, his lips met hers. The kiss started softly, and he experienced the silken feel of her. Then a passion surged through him as he bore down with an intensity that she answered. He could hear their breath louder than words, and they melted into each other's arms as he pulled her body into his. Nearly unable to stop himself, he finally tore away and held her at arm's length.

Eyes wide and almost panting, Colin stammered, "Rose, I . . . I'm . . . that was inexcusable of me."

She looked stricken. "Colin, what's wrong? Is there something wrong with me? Don't you want me?"

He frowned for a moment as he processed what she was asking. "Want you? Of course, I want you. Can't you tell? Can't you tell how much?"

She shook her head. "One minute, it feels like you're attracted to me. Then, the next minute, you seem repulsed." Her voice thickened, and her eyes teared up. "I'm so embarrassed. This is rather humiliating. I just wish it was all over." She pulled away and ran through the bushes back the way they had come. Colin quickly caught up with her.

"It's not what you think, Rose." He grabbed her arm. "Please understand." She wouldn't look up at him, so he bent over a bit to be in her sight. "Please, Rose. I find you extraordinarily attractive. Ridiculously so." He waved his arm, and she raised her eyes. "I want this to be over, too, but I want it to be over so that I'm free to take you out and actually see you like a man sees a woman." He was glad that she seemed to relax a bit. "The more time I spend with you, the more I find myself . . . wanting . . . wanting to . . . spend more time with you."

A small smile curved her lips, and her eyes brightened.

"Really?"

"Really."

"So, you meant it when you asked me to dinner . . . because you don't have to, you know. I won't hold you to it."

"Ah, but I'll hold *you* to it." He smiled.

She chuckled, and they both turned toward camp. If that kiss was a preview of what was to come, Colin was extra anxious for that dinner date.

The rest of the day at camp was unremarkable. Colin and Rose made up little competitions for themselves—who could throw a pebble closest to a target, how many twigs could each stack on top of another, which one could toast a marshmallow the darkest without burning it. These contests helped pass the time. Rose also came up with good questions. She asked what his first memory was, and he told her that he remembered his grandma crooning an old Irish lullaby long ago. Rose told him she knew a few old Irish songs and hummed some tunes until he thought she had found just the right one. Hearing that melody made him feel melancholy, but then he asked her what her first memory was.

She told him she remembered a train trip with her mother where they slept in berths in their own private room on the train and ordered breakfast in the dining car. She said she'd never forget the sound of her mother's laughter. "She always thought of fun things to do. You couldn't be bored when you were with her."

"Sort of like you, then."

Rose shook her head. "No, I'm very boring. I'm not fun like her."

"I'm having a good time."

With a scoff, Rose replied, "It's your job to have a good

time."

"No, it's my job to keep you safe, but I'm enjoying it." Colin slid back in his chair and stretched his legs. "I don't always enjoy it."

"Are you always a bodyguard?"

"No, I take on various assignments."

"Are they always dangerous?"

"It depends upon how you define dangerous."

She grimaced. "Don't be silly. The same way everybody defines dangerous, like, could you get your head shot off?"

Colin chuckled. "Then, yes, I suppose you could call the assignments dangerous—for the most part."

"What do your parents think of that?"

"Both my parents are gone."

"I'm sorry."

"It's been a few years. I've done my grieving."

"No one is ever done grieving their parents, I don't think."

Colin looked over at her. "Perhaps you're right. Some days, I feel like an orphan."

Rose got up and came over to him. She leaned down and put her arms around his neck. "You *are* an orphan, Colin," she whispered. "No matter what your age, there are moments when you're still a child." She rocked him for a moment, then kissed the top of his head.

Colin stiffened, intending to protest. He definitely wasn't a child. He was all man, always on top of things, always tough—but maybe not as tough as he insisted. He let himself soften in her arms. Her comfort felt nice. It would be easy to give in to a moment of relaxation—to allow her to soothe his overworked nerves. Colin lived on tension, alert to everything in his surroundings. Now was not the time to let down his guard.

"That feels nice, Rose, but I'm tougher than you think."

She slowly released him, then peered into his face. "I don't think so, Colin, but we'll let it go." She turned toward the coolers and pulled out some hotdogs. "How about if I get dinner started."

In a moment, they were laughing and joking, and the serious mood passed.

Chapter Nine: A Sleepless Night

After sunset, Colin tamped down the fire, and they sat listening to the night birds. Both of them were tired from the full day and the fresh air. They crawled into their sleeping bags early, and even though Colin was afraid he'd struggle to get to sleep, he faded into dreams quickly. In the morning, he awakened with Rose snuggled next to him once again. *A man could get used to this.* Of everything he was going to miss about this mission, these sleeping arrangements might be the toughest thing to part with. There was something about this trusting little body soundly sleeping right next to his that tugged at his heart. He was overcome with the desire to cover her with kisses, but he simply gave a light kiss to the top of her head. Her hair was cool and soft, and she smelled of exotic herbs. Maybe that was the scent of the brush they had hidden in yesterday. Perhaps it was the shampoo she used. He wasn't quite sure, but he could inhale it forever.

His mind was going where it shouldn't, and he wondered what it would feel like to have her hands on him. How delightful would it be to feel her sleepy touch on his thigh and up to the hardening below his waist. The thought of her soft, cool fingers wrapped around him—

Cutting that daydream off, he slid out of the sleeping bag, unintentionally jostling Rose so that her hand actually did make contact with him—right there. Blessedly, she had no idea. She rolled over and rubbed her eyes. "What time is it?"

"Almost nine." Colin rose to his feet and turned away, smoothing down the front of his pants. "I'm going to go check on the motor lodge. You can go back to sleep if you want."

She yawned. "Maybe for a little while. It's so warm and cozy in here." She snuggled down into the bag, and he glanced over. He just bet it was. He couldn't help but smile.

With a shake of his head, he forced himself out of the tent and began the walk down to the motel. As soon as he got to the car, he realized something was off. The door to their room was closed, but the *Do Not Disturb* sign was hanging with a slightly different skew on the knob.

Colin stood to the side as he pushed the door slightly. It opened without needing the key. He slipped in carefully, surveying the place for intruders. Somebody had pulled out drawers and torn things apart, but no one was there. Once he was sure the area had been vacated, he stepped back out and pulled the door closed behind him. He made his way to the registration desk. The old man sat collapsed, face down on the counter. Colin pulled him up, but he could see in a moment that the guy was gone. He hadn't been shot, but there was a massive bruise near his eye. He'd likely been whacked on the side of his face by a gun handle.

Colin spun around and took off toward the campsite. He avoided the usual trail but made his way through the trees in the thickest parts of the woods. Nearly out of breath, he burst into the tent. "Rose!"

She sat up, eyes wide, hair mussed, holding the sleeping bag up around her chest.

"We've got to get out of here."

"Why? What's wrong?"

"Just get your things together. I'll explain later."

He was glad to see her crawl out of the sleeping bag and pull her jacket on without asking any further questions. She tossed the rest of her clothes into her bag and put on her shoes. As soon as she was out of the tent, Colin collapsed the whole thing and folded it up. "Leave the cooler," he told her.

"Right now, we'll just take the tent, sleeping bags, canteens, and clothes."

She nodded, slung her purse and both canteens over her shoulder, then picked up her suitcase and sleeping bag. Colin hoisted the folded tent onto his back, then juggled his sleeping bag and suitcase in front of him. "Let's go."

Colin led Rose through the forest. They hiked silently, moving past where they had swum in the lake and where they had seen the moose. They hiked even deeper. Colin would frequently turn back and wipe out traces of their footsteps as they went. Rose began to help with that, spreading leaves out with her feet to cover their trail just like Colin did.

After a couple of hours of walking, Colin found a spot that seemed remote enough. A rather large rock flanked by an old jack pine made a sort of wall that would cover them well. He set up a small camp behind it. No fire just yet. He wanted to go back for the rest of their supplies first.

"Let me go with you, Colin."

"I don't think that's a good idea."

"I don't want to be alone here." She rubbed her arms and looked around. "There are bears in the Adirondacks. Everybody knows that."

Colin met her eyes, then nodded. "Okay, but we'll have to go very quietly."

She agreed, and they started the long trip back. Colin retraced their steps, having made various mental notes on the way up. Years of experience in the woods gave him the skills he needed to keep from getting lost. Still, making his way through this forest was taxing even for him. Eventually, they made it back to camp. They stood quietly, assessing the area before stepping out to retrieve the cooler and untie the bag of dry goods they had hung from a tree. "I think we'll just have to stash the chairs and grab them later." He folded them and pushed them behind some bushes. Then, they began the trek back to the new campsite. Both of them were thoroughly exhausted by the time they reached it. With no chairs, they sat close to each other on folded blankets.

"We started in a cabin, then moved to a motor lodge, then to a nice campsite, and now we're going primitive." Rose sighed and looked around. "What's next?"

"No tent?" Colin offered.

"So why are we here, Colin?"

"Someone found us."

"Who? And how did they find us?"

"I don't know, but it must have something to do with my phone call to Cobb yesterday."

"You think Cobb is in on it?"

"No, but someone in his office is. His phone must be bugged." Colin shook his head. "Alice, his secretary, has been sick for the last two weeks. That certainly gives me a clue."

"You need to let him know."

Colin nodded. "You're right. Plus . . ."

"Yes?"

"The old man, the one at the registration desk of the motor lodge . . ."

"Is he all right?"

"No." He sighed. "We need to alert the authorities."

"That's our fault, isn't it?" Rose's voice cracked.

"No, it's not our fault."

"Well, it wouldn't have happened if we hadn't come here. It wouldn't have happened if we hadn't entered his life—if I hadn't crossed his path with my issues—with you having to take care of me. If that hadn't happened, that man would still be alive, sitting at his desk, grinning at people and welcoming them." She was silent after that. They sat there in the cold shade of the trees. No sun could break through the heavy branches.

Colin offered Rose a sandwich from their dry goods, but

she just shook her head and gazed morosely into the shadows. She disappeared into the tent before the sun went down. He peeked in and found her sleeping. He didn't bother building a fire. He simply crawled into the tent and climbed into his sleeping bag as well.

Unfortunately, sleep didn't come as quickly tonight. Every snap of a twig or crunch of a leaf had him on edge, so he lay there, eyes open, for a great deal of the night, heart heavy and nerves frayed.

When Colin awoke, there was no warm body tucked up close to him. He sat up quickly and looked to the side. Rose wasn't in her sleeping bag. Within seconds, he was out of the tent. She was by the fire, sitting on a folded blanket and sipping coffee. "Rose?"

She looked up at him. "I woke up early. Would you like some coffee?"

"I didn't hear you."

"I was quiet. I didn't want to disturb you."

He walked over and took the cup of coffee she offered. "I'm surprised I slept through you leaving the tent."

"You tossed a little. I was afraid I woke you up."

"What time was it?"

"About four AM."

Colin looked down at his watch. "So, you've been sitting out here for two hours by yourself."

"It was peaceful."

"And lonely."

"Not really." Rose shrugged. "I'm used to my own company. Besides, I needed to think."

"And did you? Think, I mean."

She nodded. "Some."

They sat silently while Colin drank his coffee and the sun climbed to its appropriate place in the sky.

"Are you hungry," he asked her.

Rose shook her head. "How about you?"

"Not terribly." He sighed. "We've got things to take care of."

"Okay."

"We're going to go down to the car—quietly and carefully—then drive to the telephone and find out if there's any news from Cobb."

"What kind of news?"

"Well, your father may be back today. If so, you'll be returning home. If not, he'll be back tomorrow. Either way, we can't stay here. We're going back to the city, so bring what you need. We'll send agents here to retrieve the rest."

"All right." She rose to her feet.

"And, Rose . . ."

She looked down at him, long lashes casting sad shadows on her cheeks.

"It's not your fault about the old man. You can't take responsibility for the evil of others. You'll go out of your mind."

She gazed at him for a moment longer, then nodded her head. "I'll go get my things.

Chapter Ten: Her Father's Got Plans

The walk to the car was uneventful. Colin kept watch, and they went quietly, but it seemed they hadn't been tracked. Whoever had come for them must have assumed they'd left in a different vehicle. Colin started up the car and drove down the highway. He needed to get to Cobb right away.

"Colin, glad to hear from you."

"Cobb, that fruitcake you sent me last Christmas is moldy."

Cobb was quiet for a moment. Then he cleared his throat. "I'm . . . I'm sorry to hear that, Colin, and quite surprised. I'd thought it was a good sort."

"No, apparently, it wasn't the quality you thought it was."

"I see. Colin, could you call me back in about ten minutes."

"Certainly."

Colin went back to the car.

"Where are we going now? Is my father back?" Rose looked over at him.

"I don't know yet. We have to wait. I'm going to call Cobb back in ten. I have to give him time to find the bug. We have a system."

"A code?"

"Yes. He didn't know he was bugged. I gave him the code word. He's looking for it now. He'll let me know when I call back if it's clear."

Rose nodded. Colin looked over at her. He could tell she

still wasn't feeling right. Her hair was disheveled, and there were dark circles under her eyes. He understood the despair she felt. He had never been able to accept unnecessary death either. It haunted him when things like this happened. Other agents spoke of *collateral damage* and *for the greater good,* but Colin couldn't think of it that way. It would never go down easy for him. Nevertheless, it didn't affect him the way it was affecting her. He wasn't quite sure how to help her with it. He supposed each person had to deal with this kind of violence in their own way, but this was something she should never have had to experience. There were women in the organization. Some women could go out and do this job. Some were excellent and strong agents. However, a woman like Rose was too sensitive, delicate even, to face certain things—things like what Colin had to face. That was one of the reasons Colin had taken on this job—to protect people like her. Part of him felt as if he had failed this time, at least a little bit. She had been kept safe physically, but she had been harmed emotionally—on *his* watch.

Colin slid out of the car and phoned Cobb again.

"All clear, Colin. I found it. Miss Cassems, the interim secretary, is being taken for questioning."

"I'll be interested in hearing what that yields."

"Yes. I'll let you know. Now, onto the other business."

"The general."

"He'll be getting home this afternoon. You should head back there now. You can return Miss Adams safely to her father and then make your way back to London."

"Actually, Cobb, I'm going to stay on here for a few days, maybe a week or so."

"You won't need to do that, Colin. I've got a team looking into the Coalition over there. We have a few leads at this end of it here."

"Well, I may take some personal time then, a little rest."

Cobb cleared his throat. "Colin . . . you . . . uh . . . haven't found yourself . . . um . . . becoming personally involved with your charge, have you."

"Involved?"

"You know what I mean, Colin."

"Why, Cobb? It's really not your business."

"We go back a ways, Colin. Just to let you know, her father would never approve."

"Why not? What's wrong with me?"

"You're the wrong nationality."

"What do you mean? What's wrong with being British? We haven't had a fight with the States since eighteen twelve."

"Don't you know what the old man's got planned for her?"

"What do you mean—got planned for her?"

"He's grooming her to be a first lady and nothing less. The old man wants her to be a president's wife. That's why they spend more than half their year in Washington, DC. He wants his daughter to rule the White House someday."

"Doesn't it matter what *she* wants?"

"What do *you* think, old chap?" Cobb paused for a moment. "Colin . . . you're not serious about this girl, are you? You've never been serious about any woman."

"I don't know, Cobb . . . I just . . . I just want to take her out to dinner and see where it goes from there."

Cobb's voice softened. It became almost fatherly. "Well, I'd hate to see you get hurt. I'd think twice about this one, but I suppose if you want some time, take a week or so. Nevertheless, if you're going to stay there, feel free to poke around and see what you can find out about the Coalition from that side."

"Thank you, Cobb. I'll do that. And I'll keep what you say in mind. But Cobb . . ."

"Yes?"

"Fathers love me."

Cobb snorted. "Just like I do, Colin. Just like I do."

Chapter Eleven: Fathers Love Me

The drive home was quiet. Rose was glad that Colin switched on the radio. She didn't feel like chatting. It wasn't just the death of the old man that was weighing on her, although that was what had first brought her back down to earth. It was also the thought of returning home. Over the last few days, she felt like a different person. The only way to describe it was giddy, except drinking too much champagne never felt this good.

But the death of the old man smacked her face with reality. He was killed because of her, because she had come to that hotel. If Colin had picked another motor lodge—driven five miles up or stopped five miles earlier, the old man would still be alive, and some other innocent person would be dead. It was all her fault. If she had learned to take care of herself, they wouldn't have had to send somebody to protect her. But she would have never met Colin if they hadn't sent somebody. Of course, maybe that would have been better. Rose stared out the window, feeling glum. If she hadn't met Colin, she wouldn't have to feel what she was feeling now, knowing that soon he'd be leaving her at home.

Sure, he said he was going to take her out, but that didn't mean anything. Even if he really did it, he'd be going back to London, and that would be that. Besides, she was sure her father wouldn't want her seeing somebody in Colin's business. Nor would he want her to see somebody who lived so far away. Her dad always encouraged her to date men who lived in Washington. He liked her to entertain politicians and sometimes high-ranking military men. The trouble was, they were generally dull at best and horrible womanizers at worst. She would spend the evenings yawning or fighting them off. But she kept doing what her father wanted—like she always did.

Still, how could she moan about that when a man was lying dead back in the motor lodge? She should do something for his family, if he had any. Rose thought she might cry, but she fought it. She didn't want to upset Colin. He seemed concerned already. He probably thought she was a big baby now. He probably didn't even want to go out with her anymore. She wasn't being much fun now. She was being dull and morose. Why would someone like him want to go out with someone like her?

She felt a tear escape down her cheek and tried to wipe it with the back of her hand without him noticing, but she saw that he glanced over, and she turned her face away.

"Rose."

"Mmm?"

"Rose, talk to me."

She shrugged. "It's nothing, Colin. I'm just being silly."

Colin steered the car off the road and pulled to the side. He turned the key, and suddenly, everything went silent.

"Rose, look at me."

She shifted slightly to look toward him but couldn't meet his eyes. He reached out and gently took her chin to lift her face upwards. It was almost painful to look into that gaze. It was as if he was bearing down on her. She lost her breath for a moment. Then, the tears came in earnest.

"Come here." He pulled her into his arms, and she wept against his shoulder. "It's not your fault. There was nothing you could do to change it. These horrible things happen in the world." He stroked her hair as he murmured to her, "We're going to get you home, and you'll clean up, have a bath, and be in your own bed tonight, all safe and sound."

She pulled away slightly. "What about you?"

"Me?" He gave her a smirk. "I'll be in a very comfortable room at The Plaza, paid for by the bureau. Just one of the perks of doing my job."

She felt her spirits lift a bit and reached up to wipe his shirt in an attempt to dry his shoulder. "I messed up your shirt."

"I'm sure it'll be fine, but will *you* be fine? That's what I'm worried about."

She nodded. "I'm sorry. I shouldn't be such a baby."

"No, you're a beautiful, kind, and sensitive woman. I wouldn't want you any other way."

He wants me. That must mean dinner is still on. Her mood improved significantly, but she still wasn't feeling particularly talkative. The prospect of being home with Daddy was daunting. He had mentioned something about a dinner party on Friday. It wasn't like she had to do the cooking, but it was still so much work to get the place just the way he liked it. She wished she could just sit at home some Friday night and watch TV in her pajamas.

Colin carried Rose's luggage as he walked her to the door. The cook and maid were there when they reached the house, but her father wasn't home yet. Colin insisted on checking each room as well as the garage and backyard, before he would let Rose come farther than the front foyer. Then he walked through the house once again with her to make sure he hadn't missed any closet or space where someone could hide.

"I'll wait outside in the car until your father arrives. Then I'll take off. If you need anything, just let me know."

He hated to close the door behind him. He couldn't even give Rose a goodbye kiss. It wouldn't be appropriate. Simply sitting in the driver's seat, staring up at the mansion, made him feel like a pauper. Maybe Cobb was right, and he shouldn't even try to take out a woman like Rose. It was all well and good around a campfire, but now, here at her mansion, it was fairly clear that she lived a different life than what Colin could ever offer.

On the other hand, Colin made good money. He just liked to live simply. When he was on assignment, he was used to expensive and elegant surroundings—at least most of the time—but at home, he lived in a tidy, uncluttered, and very comfortable flat. Because he didn't have a lavish lifestyle, he had managed to put away quite a bit of money. If he *did* invite a woman into his life, she would be able to live nicely, but not like this. He glanced up again at the house. Rose was so comfortable in the cabin and out in the forest that it was hard to believe she really needed all this anyway.

A long black car pulled into the driveway. It stopped, and a man Colin knew to be Rose's father stepped out. The general hoisted his luggage, then took it inside. Once the door shut behind him, Colin started his car and headed toward the hotel.

After checking in, finding his room, and having a long hot shower, he called the general.

"General Adams? This is Colin Blake."

"Oh, yes. I am in your debt, young man, for taking such good care of my daughter. I can't imagine how things would have gone had she been put into the hands of those terrorists."

"I was glad to be of service. I just wanted to follow up and make sure all is well over there."

"Everything is fine, Colin, but I'm glad you called. My daughter insists that I invite you to a small dinner party we're hosting on Friday night. It's nothing big or formal, just casual evening wear. There'll be about a dozen of us."

"It would be a pleasure, sir."

"I look forward to meeting you face to face, Colin. We'll see you Friday night—about seven."

"Seven. Thank you, sir. If you should need anything before then, I'm staying at The Plaza. Please feel free to call."

"Thank you. Have a pleasant evening."

"You also."

Colin snapped his fingers. *See? Fathers love me.*

CHAPTER TWELVE: A FAKE

"I told you, Cobb, fathers love me. I'm going to a dinner party at the general's home tonight. Wish me well. Oh, hold on a second." Colin set the phone down to answer a knock at his hotel room door. It was the maid delivering his clean clothes. With a smile, he thanked her, tipped her generously, and sent her on her way. Picking up, he continued. "Sorry, Cobb. That was my laundry."

"Glad it was something so important." Cobb cleared his throat. "I could tell you were rushing back to the phone. You *do* know there was a human waiting over here, right, Colin?"

Colin laughed. "Oh, is *that* what you are, Cobb? I always wondered."

"I'm not amused, Blake."

"I apologize. I have to have my fun somehow, old man."

"I'm not that much older than you, Colin. Maybe fifteen years."

"Maybe twenty."

"Maybe." Cobb cleared his throat again. "This is a silly conversation. I don't know how I let you get me into these."

Colin chuckled. "It's my magnetic charm. I used it on the general, too."

"I doubt that, Colin. He's a strategist. He's got something up his sleeve."

"We'll see, Cobb. Whatever it is, I'm equal to it."

"Like you said, Colin. We'll see."

They said their goodbyes, and Colin left the hotel to do

some shopping. He was determined to make the best impression possible. A fine Cabernet and a bouquet of flowers would be the right choice for tonight. He considered chocolates but decided that would be too much. Flowers and a good bottle of wine would be elegant. Anything more might come across as overwhelming.

The thought of seeing Rose tonight made his heart speed up. Maybe the general *did* have something up his sleeve. Then again, perhaps he didn't. Maybe he would be glad to see Colin. After all, Colin had kept Rose safe from danger. Perhaps the general respected that and would welcome Colin to take her out. Colin hummed as he walked into the liquor store and picked out the Cabernet. He hadn't been in this good a mood for a long time.

Every time the door chimed, Rose nearly spit out her cocktail. She was on edge, waiting for Colin. She couldn't believe her father was so relaxed about her adding him to the guest list. That was a good sign. She even felt comfortable telling her dad a bit about Colin and how much fun she'd had with him. He didn't say much in return but listened and nodded. Maybe he'd be okay with her seeing him after all.

It was hard to concentrate on the chatter around her. People were used to having Rose's full attention, and she was trying, but each time a new guest showed up, she had one ear out to hear if it was Colin. At last, he arrived. She excused herself from the conversation and tried not to race across the room to greet him.

"Colin, so glad you could make it."

He handed her the wine and flowers. She accepted them, feeling a heat rise to her face. Then she kissed him on each cheek. "How thoughtful of you."

"My pleasure, Rose." He stepped back slightly and said,

"You look absolutely lovely tonight."

She knew she was blushing again, but she didn't care. She looked him up and down, laughing, and answered, "You do, too, sir."

Her father eyed them from the other side of the room, then strolled over. "So, this is the famous Colin Blake, I take it."

"Yes, Daddy. I'm so glad you're getting a chance to meet him. Colin, this is my father, General Adams."

"No, please call me Dan. No general for you, Colin, not after all you did for my daughter."

Colin gave a firm shake. "I was glad to take care of her and so glad you were able to complete your tour successfully." Colin towered over Rose's dad by at least two inches, but the general was solid and stood with an unrelenting posture that seemed to negate his congeniality. Colin exuded a relaxed confidence that almost clashed with the general's bulldog forcefulness. Nevertheless, Rose thought that the two seemed to be off to a good start.

"Rose" – the general turned to her – "why don't you go put that beautiful bouquet in some water, and I'll introduce Colin around."

She hesitated a moment, then nodded and left for the kitchen.

Once the flowers were in the vase, it was time to be seated. She walked to the table to ensure everything was in order, and the general led the group in. "Colin, you sit here by me. I want to hear all about London and what's going on there politically."

Colin glanced up at Rose but pulled out the chair next to her father's end of the table.

"And, Victoria, you sit next to Colin. We'll go boy-girl-boy-girl right down the line." He directed each person to their place. "Roger, you sit by Rose on one side. Joe, you can sit on the other side." He remained jovial as he pointed each person to their seat.

Rose wasn't surprised at who her father picked. Each man sitting next to her was an up-and-coming politician, young and popular in New York right now and destined to go places in the future—at least according to her dad. They were handsome, smart, and rich, just the kind of men her father wanted her to be with. And, of course, he'd sat Colin next to Victoria Simons, a model he had invited at the last minute, right after she had asked to invite Colin. Dad had said it was to round out the crowd.

And the gorgeous Victoria was rounding out the crowd, all right. Of course, Dad wasn't chatting with Colin. Victoria was chatting with Colin. That woman wasn't giving him one minute to turn away and talk to Dad. The general was having a long conversation with Jan Folsom on his left.

Rose bit her lip. She was afraid she might start crying. It was infuriating to watch Colin smiling and talking to Victoria. The model was gorgeous and wasn't dumb like a model should be. She was smart and poised and horrible. Rose slid her chair back. "Excuse me." She smiled. "I have to check on something in the kitchen."

When she arrived, she poured herself a glass of wine and quickly drank it. Irene, the housekeeper, came over to her. "Miss Rose, are you all right."

Rose nodded. "Yes . . . it's just . . . things aren't going as I had planned." She poured another glass of wine.

"The young man?"

"My father." She drank the second glass.

"You can't live under your father's wing all your life, miss." Irene shook her head. "He'd fire me for saying that, U suppose, but, Miss Rose . . ."

"He can't fire you, Irene. The house would fall apart." Rose smiled. "Can you imagine? I don't remember a time without you."

"Don't let your father rule your life." Irene raised an eyebrow.

Rose looked at her, then reached out and gave her a hug. "I don't know what I'd do if you weren't here with me." She swallowed, pulled away, straightened up, and took a big breath. In a moment, she returned to the table and sat back down. "All is well."

After dinner, the crowd moved into the living room. Sipping cognac and nibbling chocolates, everyone relaxed. Colin made his way over to Rose. "This doesn't count as dinner together, I hope."

"Not at all."

"So, when will you be free?"

"Is tomorrow too soon?"

"Not soon enough. We could go tonight."

Rose laughed. "If I weren't so full, I'd take you up on that, but I hope my dinner was sufficient for you."

"Very." Colin rubbed his middle. "The food was plentiful, but my time with you hasn't been."

The general wandered over toward them. "Colin, come with me. I'd like to show you my vintage firearms. A man of your persuasion would appreciate these beauties."

Colin gave a small sigh. "Certainly." He followed the general, holding his cognac and looking back at Rose.

When they entered the general's study, the general closed the door. "Look over here." The general pulled open the glass case and gave a sideways smile. "In this cabinet." He took out each piece and ordered Colin to examine and touch the collection. Colin made admiring sounds and asked a few questions. "Really nice, aren't they?" The general nodded his head and grinned.

"They are something," Colin agreed.

"Yes, I love my things and take good care of them." Colin noticed a gray steel glint deep in the general's narrowed eyes.

"I can see you do."

"I get the feeling that you're the kind of person who appreciates superior things as well." The general sat down behind his desk.

"I appreciate quality." Colin remained standing.

"Yes, I can tell that about you. And, of course, when it comes to women, I'm sure you have an eye for the finest."

"I hadn't really thought about it."

"No? One would think a man at your age, with your . . . assets . . . would have developed a certain appetite for women."

"I don't look at women as a consumable product."

"Well, women can be difficult, flighty, changeable. One day, you can be swept up, infatuated with them, and the next day, you realize you've made a mistake." The general gave Colin a pointed look. "I wouldn't want you to make a mistake, Colin."

"A mistake?" Colin cocked his chin slightly to the side. "No, I don't intend to make a mistake, sir. I assure you, there will be no mistakes. It will be one time with one woman for my entire life if I ever marry."

The general rocked a little in his chair. "Who said anything about marriage? I was just talking about mistakes. But I'm glad you said *if*. A man like you should probably not be thinking about marriage."

Colin gave a dry chuckle, then placed one finger on his chin and tapped thoughtfully. "You know, anyone would think that you don't want me to see your daughter, but that can't be, right? Because I'm the one that you said you were so happy about watching over her. That *is* what you said, isn't it?"

"Yes, that's what I said. And I'll be glad to have you here

any time she needs a bodyguard . . . just that, a *bodyguard.*"

Colin spun slightly away from the general. "Then it's good that your daughter is old enough to make her own decisions because I've already asked her to dinner, and she's accepted." He stepped toward the door. "It would have been such a shame for her to miss an elegant meal and an evening of pleasant company, wouldn't it?" He opened the door and stepped through but then turned back. "Oh, a delightful collection you have there, but the Remington eighteen ninety is a fake. Somebody cut the web of a Remington eighteen seventy-five to make it look like an eighteen ninety. The eighteen seventy-five is a more common, less valuable model, but you probably know that—you like nice things." He closed the door behind him.

Chapter Thirteen: When We Get There

Rose didn't wait for Colin to come to the door. She ran out to the car as soon as he pulled into the circular driveway.

"You should have let me call for you. I'm not afraid of your father."

Colin got out and opened the passenger door for Rose.

Rose laughed. "I didn't think you were afraid of him. I was just anxious to see you."

Taking her hand, Colin tried to help her into the car, and Rose giggled. He grinned and said, "I was anxious to see you, too. It was agonizing last night." He went back to his side and slid into the driver's seat. "You looked stunning, and I couldn't talk to you for more than five minutes."

"I felt the same way. Plus, I had to watch you with that model. My father's invite, by the way, not mine." She grimaced.

He chuckled. "I figured out what he was trying to do. But I noticed you weren't suffering for attention—a man on each side." Colin gave her a sidelong glance.

"I couldn't even hear what they were saying. I was too busy watching *you*." She leaned back in her seat. "Besides, Joe's an old friend. We've known each other since we were in diapers. That doesn't lend itself to big romance." She chuckled. "So, where are we going to dinner?"

"I was thinking maybe my hotel, The Plaza. There are several nice restaurants there. You can choose whichever one you like."

"Or we could have it sent to your room."

Colin looked over at her and then back to the street. "We could . . . but perhaps that's not appropriate."

"See? You *are* afraid of my father."

Colin scoffed. "No, I just don't want to put you in a compromising position, Rose."

"Okay. I'm sorry, Colin, but I enjoy spending time with you alone." She looked out the window. "What if we just get some hamburgers and drive someplace where there's a view?"

"Do you know a place?"

"I think so."

Watching the sparkle of the city on the Hudson River, they munched on hamburgers and rapidly cooling French fries.

"I love milkshakes," she told him, raising her cup, "but they're so bad for you."

He chuckled. "I can't remember the last time I had one." They touched their cardboard cups together then each sucked down big gulps.

"Man, that's good." Rose smiled at him.

As the evening temperature dropped, Colin turned on the car. Smooth jazz flowed out of the radio, disguising the low buzz of the heater. The wave of warm air relaxed them, and both were quiet as they ate.

Finally, they put their leftover fries up on the dashboard, and Rose slid closer to Colin. He put his arm around her, and she leaned her head against his shoulder. Colin felt solid and masculine, and his suit crunched a little against her cheek. "You smell good . . . like aftershave and cigars."

Colin laughed. "Cigars? That's not such a good smell."

"It is on *you*." She turned her head and kissed his neck, burying her face in him.

"You smell good, too, Rose." His voice was husky. He kissed the top of her head. Then he shifted so that he could gaze down at her.

Rose lifted her face, and Colin kissed her forehead, his lips gently grazing each eyelid, then traveling down her cheek. Finally, he covered her lips with his. She felt a thrill course up through her body. With almost animal pleasure, she planted small kisses around his mouth. She wanted to cover every inch of his skin, his jaw, his cheekbones. When she stopped to gaze up at him, her heart thumped. The sight of his closed eyes and his lips slightly parted was like something out of a movie. She captured his mouth with her own and plunged her tongue into him. He bore down on her in response, pulling her against him and putting a hand behind her head in order to push himself deeper. His passion was fierce, almost frightening, and definitely thrilling.

His kisses moved down her neck to the base of her throat. Then he lowered her blouse slightly to kiss down to the curve of her breasts. Rose raised her body and moaned. She wanted this. She pulled him on top of her, and she leaned back against the car door. Then she spread her legs and wrapped them around him, feeling his hardness against her. Rose had never touched a man before. She had never particularly wanted to, except with him. Now, she reached down and pushed her hand in between their bodies so that she could massage him.

Colin groaned, and his kisses grew rougher. "Rose, this is nearly unbearable." He suddenly pushed himself away and sat up. He shook his head as if coming out of a deep sleep.

Rose sat up, too. She reached over to caress the bulge that so clearly displayed his desire. How could he stop? It felt good . . . at least it did to her. Didn't it feel good to him?

Colin grabbed her hand. "No." He pulled her palm to his lips and kissed it. He continued kissing it, then moved up her wrist, up her arm, then to her lips again. Finally, he pulled back. "Not like this. Not here, not in a car. Don't you understand, Rose? It's different with you."

"What do you mean, Colin?"

"You're someone I could love . . . forever."

"Forever?" Did he mean? He hadn't known her very long, how could he? But she hadn't known him either, and she felt that way, too. She felt as if she could love him—forever. There was something about him that made her feel at home and happy.

He looked her in the eye. "I want to do it right." They sat silently for a moment. Then he continued. "I want to get down on one knee. I want to carry you over a threshold." He stopped and swallowed. "But I want to make sure you love me, too." He looked at her. "I could see myself being with you . . . as a husband . . . as a father . . . as an old man."

Rose felt her eyes fill up, and she reached for him. "I feel the same way you do, Colin. It's just scary because we met such a short time ago. Still, it seems like I can't stand being apart from you." She bit her lip. "And, Colin, I usually am not so . . . so physical . . . with anyone. Please believe me. I don't usually act like this. I've never even touched a man before."

Colin laughed. "Well, you do it like an expert."

Rose laughed, too. "Maybe you bring it out in me."

He reached up and dragged a finger down her cheek. "I want to bring out everything in you. I want to make your life wonderful. Like you, I've never felt this way before either. I've touched women, I'll admit that, but I haven't felt this way inside, not with any woman. You're right, it's scary, and I don't scare easily." Colin chuckled.

"So, what are we going to do?"

"We're going to keep seeing each other, and if we continue to feel this way, we're going to get married."

"My father will never accept it."

"We'll deal with that when we get there."

Later, after Colin had brought her home and she went to bed, Rose had difficulty getting to sleep. She tossed and turned. All she could think of was Colin's face, his body, his scent. She hoped they'd be *getting there* very soon.

Colin returned to the hotel and had two shots of brandy, one right after the other. He had as good as proposed tonight. Was he out of his mind? Yes. He was out of his mind in love with this woman. He had a feeling his life was about to change very drastically.

Well, it would be worth it. There would be a difficult road to navigate, though. Married operatives had all sorts of issues. Long times away from home, safety issues, missing important dates with the family. He'd have to discuss all that with Rose. But before he did, he'd kiss her from head to toe. Her skin was soft and had a lavender scent. He'd better stop that train of thought, or he'd need another brandy.

He let himself into his room. Maybe a cold shower would be in order. Yes, that might do the trick. He carefully took off his suit and hung everything up. The shirt would have to go back to the maid—he grinned to himself—lipstick on the collar. And Rose wore a beautiful shade of lipstick. Colin glanced over at the mirror. *Oh, great. Lipstick on the side of my cheek, too, the whole time I sat at the bar. Very dignified.* He rubbed his cheek a bit, then felt silly standing there naked, rubbing lipstick off his face. He might as well do it in the shower.

The cold water felt good against his skin, but it didn't help to get the electricity out of his body. His thoughts kept going to Rose and how their someday wedding night might look. Maybe she'd wear one of those translucent negligees. He could see himself peeling it off of her. It would slide down her shoulders, then slink to the ground, leaving her exposed, just for him. Unable to contain it, Colin gave in and touched himself, thinking about how it felt when Rose grabbed him there. What might it have been like just to continue what she wanted to do? What if he had ripped her panties off and just plunged into her right there in the backseat of the car?

Colin started breathing heavier, and he closed his eyes as he imagined it. Or what if they had come back here and had dinner in the room? Her dark hair spread across the pillow and those eyes looking up at him. Colin imagined ravaging her body, kissing each breast and exploring her secret places. He leaned back against the shower wall as his grasp moved faster. He thought about how it would feel if she was under him, if he were inside her, listening to her whisper his name, hearing her moans. Suddenly, he exploded into the flow of the shower. Pulsing with pleasure, he crumpled forward for a moment, then recovered himself.

You're acting like an adolescent. But the feeling of relaxation that came over him was worth it. He soaped up languidly. Then, after the shower, he slipped between the sheets without his pajamas. It felt exotic, but he supposed he had been acting somewhat strange these past few days, so he might as well add to it. The sheets were terrific against his skin, and he looked forward to experiencing this with Rose curled up against him in the future.

Chapter Fourteen: A Whirlwind Courtship

When Rose woke up, she lay in bed for a few moments, remembering the night before. She and Colin hadn't made plans to see each other again, so anxiety soon followed the excitement. What if he had avoided scheduling another date on purpose? What if he had actually decided *not* to see her? After all, she had been so forward, and he had made it pretty clear he desired a demure kind of woman—sexually, at least.

No. He made it even more clear he was quite interested in her. He was serious—*marriage* kind of serious.

Marriage! Her father would go out of his mind. Rose chewed her bottom lip. Well, this was bigger than her father. This was *her* life, and she wanted to spend it with Colin, at least she *thought* she did—so far. They'd have to have a little more time together, but she had a feeling her opinion of Colin wasn't going to change. He was the kind of man she could love forever. She was sure of that.

Of course, she cared what her father thought. She cared very deeply. He was the most important person in her life. Well, he had been until now. If she and Colin got married, Colin would be the most important person in her life. That was how it would have to be, and her father would need to understand that. He'd have to live with it if he wanted to remain in her life.

The jangling of the princess phone on her nightstand made

Rose jump and jarred her out of her thoughts. She grabbed it before her father could. "Hello?"

"Good morning, Rose." It was Colin's clipped British accent. Her heart gave an extra beat.

"Good morning, Colin. I had a wonderful time last night."

"I did, too." She could hear the smile in his voice. "So, when can I pick you up? I want to see you today."

Rose laughed. "You didn't even ask me out."

"It was implicit."

She laughed again. "Was it?"

"Most certainly. Every waking moment you have is now all mine. We have very little time until I leave, and we need every bit of it in order to determine if our plans to wed are good ones."

"I see. Well"—she looked around the room—"give me forty-five minutes, maybe an hour. I haven't eaten breakfast yet."

"Thirty-minutes. I'll *take* you to breakfast, and then we'll hit the museums and the park and perhaps catch a show."

"Oh, my. Thirty minutes. How will I be able to fix myself up in that short time?"

"I'm certain you are absolutely lovely even now." His voice got soft, and Rose shivered. "Are you in bed?"

"Yes?"

"Then there's no doubt about it." They were both silent for a moment. "So . . . I'll be there in thirty."

And that started what Rose could only term a whirlwind courtship—cliche as that might seem when she relayed it to her friends. Colin took her to do everything New York City had to offer. They even drove out to some of the more remote places. She was surprised by the way Colin had done his homework. He had the concierge book tickets, reserve tables, and prepare winter picnics. And the two of them explored everything. They even strolled by deserted Coney Island.

And all the while, they talked and talked.

Rose decided that for a man who did such dangerous work—and she had no doubt he frequently faced life-or-death situations—he was compassionate and thoughtful. She noticed that he was careful not to name names or give specifics, but he explained how he struggled with misgivings about some of his past missions, which troubled him as they seemed to not rise to an expected standard of ethics. It was deflating to risk one's life only to find it was for questionable purposes, he told her. But his demeanor visibly changed as she listened to him. With just one gentle stroke across his hair or a simple touch of her hand, she seemed to be able to ease his tension. Watching that made her feel valuable and vital. It warmed her to notice the furrow between his brows relax as she caressed him.

Of course, it was a joy just watching him, whether they were talking or not. The man's features drew one's eyes. He would have been a perfect artist's model. His gaze was melancholy and seductive both, and the lines of his cheeks caused shadows to fall across his face in a way that enhanced his already mysterious good looks. A mass of contradictions, his bone structure was chiseled and masculine, but his lashes were long, and his lips were lush. Nevertheless, he was totally unassuming, as if he had no idea of the effect he had on women. Still, there were moments he was so charming that Rose felt he must be aware of his magic, and she willingly fell under his spell. He moved with such cat-like grace that it was a delight to stroll the streets with him, and his gentility seemed contagious so that they made quite a striking couple. She felt unnoticeable when she was alone, but with him, she was her best self.

By the end of their week and a half, Rose was certain she would lose her grasp on happiness if Colin went back to England without her.

About the same time that Rose was thinking that, Colin was picking out a lovely diamond, simple but not tiny. He intended to present it to her on the coming evening. He had every hope that Rose would accept it.

Due to pick her up in less than an hour, he had it boxed. Then he slid it into his suit pocket and headed towards her home. He knew he was early, but he rang the doorbell. He wanted to give her father at least a chance to bless their union.

The general answered the door. "Colin." The general peered out. "Rose is not ready."

"That's fine, sir. I wanted to talk to you for a moment."

The general scowled at him. "Come in."

Colin followed the general into his study. The general sat and lit his pipe, but Colin remained standing. Colin had been in some tricky situations in the past. He had faced a plethora of frightening men, men who held his life in their hands, men who held guns at his head, who aimed rifles at his belly, yet Colin realized he was more nervous now than he had ever been then, and Colin was annoyed with himself for it. "I wanted to let you know, sir, that I intend to ask Rose to marry me this evening, and I was hoping to get your blessing."

The general peered up at him and took a few puffs of his pipe. "Colin . . . if she marries you . . . I will completely disinherit her. She will not get a single cent from me." The general shook his head. "Don't expect to live like this, Colin." He spread his arm out.

Colin could feel his face heat and his fists clench. "I would never expect to live off my wife's money. I will be the sole support of my family and hadn't even thought about any inheritance Rose might have." He walked around the desk and leaned down over the general. "Whatever you might think of me, whatever reasons you may have for not wanting me to marry her, I am extraordinarily offended that you would suggest such a thing." Colin straightened up and took a long breath. "I withdraw my request for your blessings, sir, but be aware that I certainly am going to ask your daughter to marry me, and when I marry her, I hope to take her away from this place where both she and I are so extremely underestimated." Colin watched the general's jaw drop slightly. Then he turned and quickly walked out of the study. Rose was waiting on the other side of the door, looking dismayed. Colin grabbed her arm and escorted her through the front door and into the car.

Chapter Fifteen: The Question

Once they were in the car, Colin sat for a moment to compose himself, and he felt Rose's eyes on him. "My father offended you," she said.

Colin nodded. "Yes." He waited for a moment, then added. "You should know, Rose, that he intends to disinherit you if you marry me."

"What? Oh, Colin." She reached for him. "I don't care about that. I don't care about the money. You didn't think I would change my mind, did you?"

Part of him remembered her at the dinner party, sophisticated and elite. Although he was glad to be marrying someone who could handle those types of things, he wouldn't have the funds to throw lavish parties, and he supposed he did worry a bit about what she might expect.

"No, I didn't think that." He shook his head. "But you should have the choice." He turned towards her. "It's your right to have the lifestyle you want. It's not my place to steal that from you."

Her eyes glistened. "You're giving me something that all my father's money could never buy. I've always preferred to live more simply. Do you think I really enjoy all . . . this?" She waved her hand. "I may host parties and plan social events, but I only do that for *him*. I don't have fun doing that. It's all for his sake."

Colin pushed his arms around her, and they sat close for a few minutes. She was soft but solid, womanly. Her body was a physical representation of who *she* was—gentle but with a core of stability he felt he could rely on, even lean on. With that, he pulled back and started the car. He headed toward the place that looked out over the Hudson, where they had eaten burgers the week before. After parking the car, he got out and came around to open the door for her. Rose looked confused, but she got out.

Colin held both her hands and looked down at her. The wind coming off the water lifted her hair, and the night sky lit her eyes. He thought she had never looked so beautiful. No one in his life had ever seemed so enticing yet so pure, and his heart felt as if it would burst and pour over.

He dropped to one knee and looked up at her. "Rose Adams, will you please do me the honor, the incredible blessing, of taking the rest of life's journey with me and becoming my wife?"

"Oh, Colin." She gave a little moan and dropped to her knees to face him. Tears began to flow as she melted into his chest. "Of course I will. I have never been so happy in my life. I love you with all my heart, all my being. I'll be by your side forever."

Colin dug the ring out of his pocket. He was pleased at Rose's gasp. "It's beautiful!" Then he slid it on her finger. She held her hand up and admired the sparkle in the moonlight. "When shall we get married?" she asked.

"Well, that's up to you." Colin rose and helped Rose to her feet. "What kind of wedding would you like?"

"I would be fine with a small one. In light of my father's attitude, perhaps we should simply marry at City Hall with a few of my friends."

"You don't want a white gown and chapel wedding?" Colin gazed into her eyes.

"Well, of course I do. Every girl wants the dream wedding, but it's just not feasible, Colin. Daddy won't pay for it, and I don't want to be apart from you long enough to plan it."

"Are you sure?"

"I'm absolutely sure."

"Okay, I have to get back to London, but if we get blood tests tomorrow, we could marry in four days."

"That's perfect. I'll call a few friends and make some arrangements. Can you book me a room at your hotel for the night before? I don't really want to have to deal with Daddy then."

"Certainly. What else can I do?"

"Pick me up for the blood tests in the morning and I'm sure I'll have a list for you." She smiled, and Colin laughed.

"Already? Am I in for trouble once we've tied the knot?"

"I run a tight ship, Colin Blake. You wait and see."

He looked forward to it, but then he wondered how she would feel about his flat. She would probably want to move. That caused a whole new flow of anxiety. *I'll worry about that later.* But the things he hadn't dealt with yet, like warning her about his lifestyle and what she'd be facing as an operative's wife, along with wondering how she'd do with living in a whole new country, apart from her friends and family—those things—they were eating away at him a bit.

Chapter Sixteen: A Celebration

Rose broke the news to her father over breakfast. It was easier than she thought it would be. She had been afraid that she would shrink under his glares and threats, but she didn't. When he went silent, though, it was tough. Almost childishly, he wouldn't answer even the simplest of questions. *Do you want jelly with your toast?* He simply stared right through her. And that was how the next few days went. No *good mornings*, no hugs goodnight, it was as if she didn't exist for him. She thought he'd get over it, and she even kept talking to him up until the moment she finally picked up her bag and went out the door to get in Colin's car. Still, her father didn't relent. This was his way of saying she was dead to him.

His treatment hurt at first. She had a hard time sleeping, tossing and turning with guilt, but after a day or so, she felt anger creep in. Why did he have to be so stubborn? He wasn't even willing to have a conversation about her reasons. It was her life, and she should at least have some say over who she married. But he seemed unprepared to give even an inch.

After putting her things in the trunk, Colin let her in the passenger side of the car. She had a lovely dress for the wedding ceremony but certainly not a big white gown. Still, it was enough. She was glad to be marrying Colin. It was the marriage that mattered, not the ceremony.

"How is your father? Any better?"

She shook her head. "Not a bit. I have no one to give me away," she answered morosely.

"He doesn't want to part with you, Rose. I can't say I blame him." He smiled over at her. "I wouldn't want to part with you either."

Rubbing his arm, she assured him that would never happen. She was relaxing already. Just being near Colin put her more at ease.

They got to The Plaza. Colin had booked her the room across the hall from his. He gave the bellboy a generous tip, then turned to Rose. "Is this good enough for you? After all, you *are* getting married tomorrow."

Rose looked around. "It's beautiful . . . *and* it's right across the hall from you. That makes it all the better."

"Are you hungry?"

She shook her head. "Not very, but I suppose we should have a little something. Do you want to order room service?"

"That'd be fine . . . a quiet dinner." Colin got on the phone and requested a light meal. Then he sat down in a plush chair across from her bed. "Are you nervous?"

Rose kicked off her shoes, then scooted back on the bed and leaned against the headboard. "Maybe a little." She grinned and pulled her knees up in front of her. "I've never been married before."

"Nor have I." He shook his head. "I never thought I would. What have you done to me?"

"What have *I* done? *You're* the one with all the magic."

"Is that so?" He got up and sat down on the bed facing her.

"That's how it feels to me."

Colin reached over and ran his finger down her leg. Rose shivered. "See?" she said. "That's magic . . . your touch."

"And so is yours." His voice was low.

"Is it?" Rose reached over and dragged a fingernail over the leg of his pants. "Does that do anything?"

Colin grinned. "You're playing a dangerous game, young lady."

"With fire?"

"With fire."

They leaned into each other, but a knock came on the door just as their lips were about to meet. "Room service," a low voice droned.

Rose reluctantly allowed Colin to pull himself away. He answered the door, and a smiling bellboy rolled in the cart. The bellboy lifted warmers off the plates, then uncorked a bottle of wine, pouring a little in each glass. "Anything else, sir?"

"No, thank you." Colin tipped him and saw him out the door.

Once the bellboy was gone, Rose sat up and patted the place next to her on the bed. Colin and Rose sat side by side, nibbling at their food. Rose could feel the wine going to her head. She lifted a fork full of potatoes to Colin's mouth. "Here"—she laughed—"practice for wedding cake tomorrow." He gobbled her offering, making silly noises, then kissed her hand, then her wrist, then down her arm, all the while pretending he was eating her up. She fell back on the bed, giggling.

"Mmmm," he said, "the best dessert in the entire hotel." He nuzzled her neck and kissed her ear.

Rose dropped the fork and put her arms around him. She needed to feel his lips against hers, wanted to inhale him, have more of him. Her breath grew deeper, and her body began to rise. She felt him respond. He pressed against her, and she could feel his excitement grow. His kisses became more frantic, and when he put his mouth over hers, his tongue was probing and insistent.

She couldn't help herself . . . didn't want to help herself. She reached for his shirt and began to pull the buttons apart. He didn't stop her, but she saw the frown on his face.

"Rose," he began, but she reached up and put a finger over his mouth.

"It's tomorrow," she whispered. "What harm could it do to

have each other tonight?"

"We should wait— " But she cut off his words by lifting her mouth to his. She kept working away at his shirt while quieting him with a deep kiss. Once she undid the buttons, she almost violently pushed the shirt off his shoulders, and he allowed her to tug the sleeves the rest of the way down until they were entirely off.

"Rose . . . " His voice wavered.

She yanked his t-shirt up from his trousers, then ran her hands over the warm skin of his belly, her fingertips just tracing the lines under his belt. Colin drew in his breath.

"You are making this very difficult." He stammered, "I can't . . . I can't . . ."

She unbelted, then unbuttoned his pants and snuck her hand in, trying to touch him. When she reached her prize, she held him tightly and began to explore. Colin moaned, raised himself up, then fell onto his back. "What are you doing to me?"

"I want to see you. I want to have you, Colin. I can't wait." She barely recognized herself at this point. She felt ravenous. Straddling him, she pulled his t-shirt over his head. Colin looked up at her with wide eyes, so blue and beautiful it made her belly twist. Then she leaned down and began covering him with kisses—all over his chest and stomach, enjoying the sounds of his moans.

"All right, all right," he gasped, "have it your way." He pushed her to the side, then rose off the bed and kicked off his pants. "You need to know exactly what you started," he told her with a gleam in his eyes.

He came back to the bed and tore off her blouse. She felt his kisses all over the top of her breasts. He was torturing her—she needed more. She grabbed his hair and held him closer, raising her back from the bed. Colin reached behind her and unfastened her bra, then pulled it off. He whispered something she could barely comprehend about how beautiful she was. Then he did things with his mouth that made her feel like she would lose her mind. She couldn't help but wrap her legs around him and urge him to take her, but he held back.

At last he worked her skirt off her, then slid her panties down to her ankles. She kicked them off. He gently grazed the tender spot between her legs, causing an earthquake of emotional and physical reactions. She hadn't known it was possible to feel like this. As his touch became more intense, sounds that would have been embarrassing if she had cared came from her. Then, finally, he positioned himself over her and tenderly began to thrust, slowly at first, then faster as she encouraged it.

He went deeper and deeper until Rose felt as if they were one. It was a profound feeling—a feeling of unity, a giving of herself. This was an expression of love like no other. Colin stroked her hair and whispered, "Look at me, Rose."

She opened her eyes and gazed up into his face as they joined together, gently, then faster, then with such passion that she had to squeeze her eyes shut again in order to endure the joy. Still, when she forced herself to look for a moment, she saw his head thrown back, an expression of ecstasy on his face, as he turned from side to side and released into her.

When they had finished, they lay there, his weight totally upon her. "I suppose I'm crushing you," he said.

"I want you to crush me," she answered.

He gave a small chuckle, then rolled to the side and pulled her into his arms. "This might be more comfortable for you."

When they finally pulled themselves out of bed, Rose felt elated. "I'm going to order some champagne."

Colin laughed at her. "Celebrating?"

"Of course." She came over and gave him a kiss. "That was the most remarkable thing that ever happened to me."

"Uh oh. Setting a high bar for me."

She reached over and mussed his hair. "Don't be ridiculous. You set the high bar for yourself." With a laugh, she bounced over to the phone and called down to the kitchen to order the champagne. "Let's jump in the shower before it gets here."

Colin was ever the gentleman and soaped her up first so that she could hop out of the shower, get dressed, and be ready for the bellboy's knock. This was the happiest day of her life, or at least it would be, until tomorrow, then *that* would be the happiest day of her life—the day they would marry.

Rose hummed a tune as she dried herself off and threw a light shift on. She was halfway through putting her hair in a braid when the champagne arrived, and she went to the door to let the bellboy in—only it wasn't the bellboy.

The first thing she saw was a big black revolver. Then she saw the man's face. It was a cruel face. At least, that was her thought as she assessed it. Two men pushed their way in. Immediately, one had his hand over her mouth. He whispered, "Don't make a noise, or we'll have to start shooting up the place." He raised his chin toward the bathroom. "And we'll start with whoever's in that shower." He looked back into Rose's eyes. "You wouldn't want *that* on your conscience, would you?"

Rose quickly shook her head.

"Good." He nodded to his partner. "Get her coat, and let's get out of here." The other guy grabbed her coat, and Rose was dragged out of the room and down the hall of The Plaza. The men wrangled her into a car and put a bag over her head.

Chapter Seventeen: Then Everything Went Black

The drive was surprisingly short. Then Rose felt herself yanked from the backseat. She was dragged down some stairs. Doors clanged, and light filtered through the material covering her head. The men pushed her onto a hard chair and pulled her arms behind her.

"Ow." She struggled, but they told her to hold still and tied her wrists together with what felt like a thick rope. "What's this all about?" She tried not to sound frightened, but her heart was pounding in her ears.

"Be patient." One of the men whispered in her ear, "The boss will be with us shortly, and he'll make everything crystal clear." He snickered and ran what felt like a finger along her knee. Rose jerked away. "Oh"—he grabbed her leg—"you only sleep with British agents, huh?" He laughed when she didn't answer.

Rose heard him pull away and walk to the other side of the room. The men spoke too softly for her to make out what they said. She silently sat while they talked, but she pulled at the rope binding her wrists as she did. It was bulky. Maybe if she pulled enough, she'd be able to work her hands out. It was slow going, and the rope cut into her wrists, but she was making progress. She was sure of it.

One of the men was clearly becoming unhappy with the lengthy delay. "How long did he say he was going to be? I don't like this."

"Any minute. You'll get your money, just . . . " But his voice grew too quiet to hear more.

Rose was just as happy about the wait. This gave her more time to try to twist her wrists through the knots. She was sure she was bleeding, but she didn't care. After a while, though, she heard the sound of a door opening and closing.

"Boss."

A mechanical, reverberating noise cut through the air. "Good job, men."

The boss's voice sounds robotic.

"Thanks, boss."

"Good evening, Miss Adams. We have a few questions for you," the odd voice continued.

Rose said nothing but kept carefully working away at the ropes.

"We need to know a few things about Mr. Blake and suspect you know quite a bit about the man."

"Nothing that would interest you." She tried to keep her voice from wavering.

"Let us be the judge of that. You just tell us what he has discussed with you about any of his past, present, or future jobs."

"He's a travel agent. There's nothing much to say."

If Rose thought the voice was odd, the laugh was even more mechanical. "Oh, my, I think we *both* know better than that, Miss Adams. Now, don't make me hurt you. Let's keep this civilized."

Don't panic . . . don't panic . . . If her struggle with the ropes became too obvious, they'd immediately come over and tighten them. Then she'd have no chance.

"What kinds of things has Mr. Blake shared with you? Certainly, in all your time together, something about his work has come up."

She called out, "Nothing . . . nothing of any substance. He's more professional than that."

"Hmmm . . . then we're just going to have to use you as bait and find out what we need straight from him."

Rose's heart dropped. "Well, I can tell you a few things."

"That's encouraging."

Rose pulled at the ropes.

"Hey, what are you doing over there?" She heard one of the men come toward her. He grabbed her shoulders, but her hands were loose by that time. In an amazing stroke of luck, as she lashed out against him, her right hand brushed against something metallic, and she grabbed it. She knew from the feel of it that it was a gun. She began shooting blindly, first at the man who held her, and then she shot toward the place where the odd voice was coming from.

Pandemonium broke out. She heard the doors open, voices shouting, and feet running. Someone grabbed her arm. She continued to pull the trigger wildly.

"Stop. Stop, Rose. It's all right." *Colin's here.* She reached up and pulled the bag off her head. Then she fell into his arms, sobbing.

He held her closer and kissed her head. "It's okay, sweetheart. The police are here with me." She finally began to pull away and turn to see her captors, but Colin grabbed her and said, "Wait."

"Why?" Had she killed those people she shot at? What had she done? With a jerk, she turned from him to survey the room. An intimidating looking brute was being bandaged up by a policeman. Rose had a feeling that was the man who had tied her to the chair. Then, in a shadowy end of the cellar, behind a table, two other policemen were holding someone who was facing away from her. His arm was bleeding. Clearly, she had shot him. There was audio equipment on the table where he stood. That must have been what he used to alter his voice. The men led him out from behind the table and into the light. Colin caught Rose as her knees buckled. "Daddy?" She looked up at the general.

Her father looked back at her with pleading eyes. "I just wanted you to realize how dangerous it would be to marry him."

Rose shook her head, bewildered. "I don't understand."

"I was trying to keep you safe . . . to give you an idea of what could happen."

"But I shot you." Rose stared at his bleeding arm. Then everything went black.

CHAPTER EIGHTEEN: THE RIGHT THING

Colin held Rose in his arms as she slept. Once his fingers began to tingle, he carefully slid from her and sat up against the headboard. He had rarely had a night as emotionally charged as this.

First, there was the delicious intimacy of making love to her. He glanced down at her tousled hair as he savored that memory. She had been wild but sweet, everything a man could want in a woman and more. There had not been a trace of sophistication in her approach to sex. All her reactions were naive but primal. This was novel and thrilling for him. But then, he had emerged from the shower to find the room empty.

At first, he had thought she was upset. He discarded that idea immediately. She had seemed too genuinely delighted. Then he thought she had gone into the hallway and locked herself out, but there was no sign of her. It only took a few minutes to realize she had been taken.

Of course, Colin had called Rose's father immediately to enlist his help in locating her, but the maid said the general had gone out. Colin needed to find the general and let him know Rose was missing. Colin had connections in the police force, and they put out an APB on the general's car. Once the car was located, Colin went to join the squad that waited there. When they heard shooting, they burst in. Colin was stunned to see Rose, head covered, waving a gun wildly and shooting into the air. She almost hit one of the policemen. Colin had to creep up beside her to get her to stop. When he saw that the general was the culprit and that Rose had shot him, he didn't want her to turn around, but it was too late. She twisted away. At least she had only shot her father in the arm.

He knew she was shocked, but he hadn't expected her to lose consciousness. He supposed he shouldn't have been so surprised. When she came to, she trembled so fiercely that he practically had to carry her to the car. And when he finally got her home, he gave her three glasses of brandy. That settled her down. Then he held her until she slept. She didn't speak a word. She simply looked at him with wide eyes—well, looked *through* him more like.

Colin sighed as he watched her sleep. He pulled out a cigarette, then leaned back and smoked it. What a mess he had made of this woman's life—and of the general's life, too, he supposed. Until Colin came along, they'd lived quietly and had a bright future mapped out. Rose probably would have been a first lady. Of course, she wouldn't have been terribly happy. But what kind of happiness was she going to have now—now that her father was going to be facing kidnapping charges? He let out a long cloud of smoke. The general made a terrible mistake, but he was right about one thing. Rose would be in great danger if she married Colin. One day he might come home from work and find her missing, and she wouldn't be as safe as she had been when she was sitting in front of the general who had been pretending to be a *bad guy*.

Colin stubbed the cigarette out. He really should have thought this through more carefully. *Who risks the life of someone they love so dearly?* He looked back down at Rose. Her hair covered part of her face. Using two fingers, he gently pushed it back. She moaned slightly and wriggled closer to him. *Look at her, so trusting and vulnerable. She could easily end up dead because of me.*

Well, he couldn't back out right now. She would need him in the morning. He'd have to think things over, though . . .

maybe return to England without her and then see how things went. This whole marriage endeavor was so foolhardy. He was going to need to be tougher. He'd help her through this difficult time, then make sure she was safe. He needed to act in her best interests, not his own.

Colin bit his lip and swallowed. Then he slid back down into the bed and held Rose close. It didn't matter how much it hurt. He had to do the right thing. He squeezed his eyes shut and sniffed, then kissed her hair. She nuzzled him in her sleep, and he felt as if his heart would tear in two.

CHAPTER NINETEEN: WORTH THE RISK

Colin shook hands with Norm Hopkins, Rose's family attorney. He was a middle-aged man who reminded Colin of his own solicitor back in London. Norm took a seat behind his large mahogany desk while Colin and Rose sat across from him.

"I'm so sorry, Rose, about everything that has transpired." Norm shook his head and frowned.

"I'm not going to press charges, of course."

"Rose . . . " Norm tapped the desk with his pen. "It's not a matter of you pressing charges. Your father broke the law. The state is pressing charges against him."

Rose leaned forward and answered Norm. "Well, you'll just have to defend him, Norm. You know he was not acting like himself." Colin could hear the desperation in Rose's voice.

"I'm not a criminal lawyer, Rose."

"Well then, hire the best lawyers there are. He can afford whoever you can get." She stood up.

Colin stood with her and put his hands on her shoulders. "Rose, sit down and let Norm finish. I'm sure he has some good advice for you."

Norm nodded up at them. "Yes, Colin. I have some important things to share with Rose. I'm not sure, Rose, if you want Colin to stay."

Rose turned toward Colin. "Well, of course I do. He can hear whatever you have to tell me." She lowered herself back in the chair. Colin pulled his chair a little closer to her and kept his hand on her arm.

"Your father has very little money, Rose. He only has his pension, and he hasn't saved any of it. He's spent it on a very lavish lifestyle."

"So, we'll sell some things . . . we'll sell the house."

Norm cleared his throat. "The house doesn't belong to him."

"It what?" Rose abruptly leaned back in the chair.

"You see, your mother was the one that brought all the money into the marriage, and when she died, she left everything to you in a trust fund, of which your father was the trustee. You have full rights of withdrawal at age thirty. The house is held in your name . . . in the name of your trust, but you are the beneficiary. Of course, after this incident, your father can no longer serve as trustee." Norm looked apologetic. "And I can no longer act as his legal representative."

"Well, he can sell the home in DC then and use the proceeds from that."

"I'm afraid that's yours, too."

"And the one in Martha's Vineyard."

"Also yours. Everything is yours, Rose."

"I don't want it. I want my father to be protected." Her voice went up a few notches. "What can I do? Who's the trustee now?"

"I am the successor trustee of your trust, and it's my fiduciary duty to see that the funds are used in your best interest."

Rose stood up and leaned over the desk. Her fist hit the mahogany top with a resounding thump that nearly made Colin jump. "Well then, you'd better see that it's in my best interests to get my father out of this trouble, Norm, or I'll see that it's in my best interests to find another trustee—some way, somehow. Do you understand?"

Norm leaned back and batted his eyes a few times. "Yes, ma'am."

"I want to see what I've got in what accounts, and I want you to liquidate something to come up with the money to retain the best attorney to represent my father."

Norm nodded. "Okay. I'll get it done. But you need to be reasonable, Rose."

"No, I don't need to be reasonable. I need to be effective. My father needs to be out of jail and back home as soon as possible."

"All right."

Rose turned to Colin. He couldn't help but be impressed with her performance, but as soon as they returned to the car, she leaned forward with her face almost down to her lap and she began to sob. He reached for her and pulled her close. "I didn't ask for any of this, Colin. I didn't want it." She shook her head as she cried.

"I know, I know, shhhhh." And he stroked her hair as he calmed her. He just needed to stay with her a little longer and *then* he would return to London. He couldn't leave her now . . . not like this.

It had been a week since the visit to Rose's lawyer, and she seemed to have collected herself. When she dealt with Norm, she was a powerful woman, calling the shots and telling him what to do, but Colin knew inside that Rose was feeling delicate. He wished he could do more to help her with the grief of learning the true character of her father. Here she was trying to rescue him, as if she were the parent and he was the child. Still, she was rising to the situation, and Colin thought it might now be the right time to fly home.

She was already going through so much, and he felt like a heel deserting her, but how much good would it do to keep clinging to her and raising her expectations only to let her down later? He had accepted that he couldn't drag her into a treacherous marriage to him. Her life would be constantly in danger. But he knew she would never agree to end it for that reason. He would just have to fade from her life. She would be swept up with everything here and maybe just forget about him.

"Rose?" He approached her gently. "We have to talk."

"You've got to return to London." It wasn't a question. She looked at him with no light in her eyes and no smile on her face.

Colin nodded.

"I knew it. I could tell."

"What do you mean?"

She shook her head. "You don't think I could feel you withdrawing from me more and more every day, Colin?" A tear trickled down her face. "Not that I blame you. Who would want to marry into a family like this? And I'm a mess." She wiped her cheek with the back of her hand.

"No, Rose. You don't understand."

"Here." She pulled the engagement ring off her finger. "I *do* understand. I won't hold you to this."

"Rose . . ."

"Take it."

"I don't want the ring. You keep it." Colin turned away. Then he turned back. "I just want you to be safe, Rose. That's more important than anything else."

"Is it, Colin?" She gave him a long look. "I just wonder . . . because I'm very safe right now, and it certainly doesn't *feel* important at all. You know when I was happiest?"

Colin shook his head.

"When my life was in danger, in that cabin, at the motor lodge, up in the forest—when I was the least safe. Ironic, isn't it? I'm not really sure how valuable safety really is." She turned away. "Irene will see you out. I wish you the best." Colin watched her walk up the stairs and disappear into the second floor. Colin saw himself out. He didn't need Irene, and he certainly didn't want to catch the disapproving looks the maid would surely give him.

He headed to the car, went back to the hotel, and packed. The sooner he could get to London, the better. He was a mass of pain, nerves, and guilt. Was she right? Might it be better to take the risk just to be happy? *No, don't be ridiculous – to risk her life . . . what if she ended up dead?* But he wondered.

Chapter Twenty: It Suddenly Occurred to Her

Just when Rose needed him most, Colin was gone. Because of his position, her father's trial was expedited. From the first day, Rose found herself escorted into the courthouse by faceless men, fending off the popping flashbulbs and reporters shouting questions at her. By the second week, she awakened in the morning, her stomach in knots. She crawled into her bathroom and bent over the toilet, throwing up until she thought her knees would buckle. Irene brought her tea and dry toast, then sat with her, helping to prepare her for what the day was going to bring.

Watching her father in court made Rose's heart break. He was a defeated man. Once proud—way too proud—and strong, he sat bent over and ashamed, eyes lowered and voice quiet. He stammered out that he had only been trying to show his daughter how dangerous it could be to marry a man like Colin, but he was laughed at. After all, Colin was only a travel agent, wasn't he? At the same time, Colin was labeled a jet-set playboy, out to marry Rose for her money. Rose looked foolish for falling for him. The whole thing was humiliating. In the end, Rose felt as if she had lost her father, lost her lover, lost her dignity, and possibly her mind.

She tried to cover the circles under her eyes with makeup but knew she looked awful, and the photographers loved it. What did they expect? It was painful knowing that strangers were out there watching, judging, maybe even gleeful about her predicament, about everything that went on.

People who used to vie for party invitations or beg her to show up at their events had deserted her, not that she cared much about that, but with Colin gone, she certainly wished she had somebody to support her, even just a little.

Into that emptiness stepped Joe West, and she was grateful for him.

"Rose, how are you holding up?" His voice was warm on the other end of the phone.

"It's not easy, Joe. I'll be honest. I really appreciate you calling."

"Would you like some company at the courthouse?"

From then on, he came with her each day and then had dinner with her every night. He was assertive with the press and quite protective of her. Rose could sometimes relax and let him take care of her. There were moments, however, that his behavior made her ache for Colin—much as she tried to shake Colin from her head.

Everything to do with the trial seemed to drag on. After six weeks of being on display, she didn't know how much more she could take. She was sick every morning and exhausted to the core. She had never been so tired in her life. Her system was so beat up that she stopped having her period . . . then it suddenly occurred to her . . .

"Colin, this thing is a mess. It's a scandal." Cobb looked up from his paper.

"I know, Cobb." Colin paced back and forth across the office.

"Your cover is blown, not directly, but things certainly will be obvious to those who have suspicions. You're of no use to MI6 right now."

"So? What then? Retire? Quit?"

"Don't be ridiculous, nobody quits MI6." Cobb shook his head. "I've made a few inquiries, and it looks like NATO can use you for a while."

"NATO?"

"Yes. We're transferring you to Brussels to work with them as an accountant."

Colin scoffed. "I know I'm good with numbers, but I hardly see myself sitting at a desk every day—"

Cobb cut him off. "As an accountant on record, but they have some tasks you will take care of from time to time—things that are not in the ordinary job description for accountants . . . or any other job title, for that matter."

"Really?" Colin's eyebrows lifted.

"It's a unique position not on the books . . . not many even know it exists."

"I certainly didn't know it existed."

"You don't know everything, Colin."

"What else don't I know?"

Cobb ignored the question. "You'll report to New York—the United Nations Building—next Monday for a series of briefings. We're giving you a few days to arrange with administration to have your flat subleased and get your things packed. NATO will have a temporary apartment for you in the city. I'm sure it will be satisfactory." Cobb gave a slight smile. "After a month in New York, you'll be transferred to NATO headquarters in Belgium, but don't worry, you'll be back in London eventually, when all this blows over. It'll take some time."

Colin nodded, then started to leave. He turned back momentarily. "Thank you, Cobb."

It had been over two months since Colin had left New York and said goodbye to Rose, but it seemed like the scent of her still lingered on his pillow at night, even if she had never been in his bed. His heart raced a little as he prepared for the move to New York, and by the time his plane landed, he had decided that maybe the accounting job at NATO would end up being a great cover. Maybe he could see Rose again and they could talk about a future—maybe. Then again, maybe it would still be foolhardy.

During the entire flight, his emotions tormented him. One minute, he felt as if he was missing a part of himself, an almost physical pain that would only be resolved if he could hold Rose against his chest. The next minute, he would tighten his fists and remember the horror that struck him when he realized she had been taken from the hotel room.

He wasn't able to sleep, read, or relax during the flight, but he hadn't been able to do any of those things much since he left her. He had seen her pictures in the paper. She looked lost. If he could have been there for her, to comfort her and care for her . . . but he was sure that would have only made things worse. Still, looking at her suffer like that was killing him.

After touching down at Idlewild, he caught a cab. Part of him wanted to go straight to Rose, but that would be too impulsive. Colin was not an impulsive man—his nails dug into his palms as he clenched his fists and reminded himself of that. *Impulse gets you in trouble. Everything must be well thought out.*

He got to the apartment building, tipped the cab driver, then got his luggage upstairs. The Tudor City apartment was beautiful. He had to give NATO credit for providing a lovely residence. There was a wonderful view of the city. The apartment was beautifully furnished, and it was pristinely cared for. He wanted to bring Rose up here and give her a look at this view. He needed to see her. It was hard being this close to her. He shook his head, then went out the door, down the elevator, and out to a cab.

In spite of a few misgivings, Colin stepped out of the cab when they reached Rose's circular driveway. He tipped the driver and let him go, but then he stood in front of the entrance door for a long time before ringing. Finally, he stretched his fingers out and took a breath before reaching for the bell. It took a few moments and then Irene opened up and looked out at him. With a scowl, she said, "Oh, *you*. What do *you* want?"

"May I come in?" Irene opened the door, and Colin stepped into the foyer. "I came to see Rose." He spoke more confidently than he felt.

"She's out."

"Do you know when she'll be back?"

"She's out with her new fiancé." Irene crossed her arms over her chest and scowled.

Feeling as if somebody had just punched him in the solar plexus, Colin felt his knees buckle and fell sideways against the wall. Irene's face changed as she reached out to steady him. He pulled away from her, then straightened up. His eyes suddenly felt puffy. Clearing his throat, he swallowed and pushed his shoulders back. "Well, it didn't take her long to move on, did it?"

"What choice did you give her?" Irene's lips turned downward. "You could have at least taken her to London and married her. You could have given her a quiet divorce after that. But no, you had to desert her."

Colin shook his head. "I don't understand. Why would I have married her only to give her a divorce?"

"Shame on you," she said, closing her eyes and shaking her head. "You had your fun and then you were gone. It wasn't her money you were after. It was her innocence. That's even worse."

"It wasn't like that, Irene."

"Well, now, she's got somebody who actually *will* care for her and for her baby, in spite of her circumstances. That's *real* love, Mr. Blake. So you needn't bother yourself with her. Just go away and leave her in peace like you wanted to in the first place."

For the second time, Colin found himself against the wall. "The baby?"

Irene's eyes widened. "You didn't know?"

"Of course I didn't know. Do you think I would have left if I had known?" Colin straightened up. "And for the record, Irene, the only reason I left is because I wanted Rose to be safe. I love her. Being married to me, with my job—Irene"—he shook his head—"I love her. I loved her then. I love her now."

"Well, she's engaged." Irene reached into her pocket and pulled out a newspaper clipping, then handed it to Colin. *Rose Elaine Adams to wed Joseph Henry West.* His hand shook as he looked at the photo of the two of them. Joe's hand rested protectively on Rose's shoulder, and his eyes sparkled, but there was no smile in *her* eyes.

"She doesn't love him."

Irene shook her head. "But she's engaged, and *he* loves *her.*"

"Still, she doesn't love him."

"She *will,* and he'll take care of her and the child. Go away, Colin. Leave her alone. You've done enough damage to this family."

Colin looked up at her, clipping still trembling in his hand. *His* woman, *his* child . . . how could he part with them?

Chapter Twenty-One: His Woman, His Child

Colin dropped the clipping and stumbled out the front door. He could barely see as he staggered down the circular drive and out to the street. Somehow, he managed to flag down a cab and get back to his new apartment. He held everything inside until the door was closed and bolted. Then he fell face down on his bed, holding back sobs. The bitterness was unbearable. He rolled to his side, trying to disappear inside himself. This was worse than any torture he had endured at the hands of an enemy, and it seemed like it would go on forever. No matter how much he chided himself or told himself to man up, he felt tears pushing at his eyes and sounds building in his throat. The echoes in his heart were almost frightening. After what must have been nearly two hours, he struggled to his feet and staggered to the mirror. His eyes were red, and his face was blotchy. Leftover emotions hiccupped out of him as he surveyed the blurry mess that stared back. He couldn't remember ever crying in his adult life and almost laughed at the ridiculous sight that stared back at him as he battled the tears now.

Shaking himself, he stumbled out to the living room and searched the cabinet behind the oak bar. NATO had kindly supplied him with Chivas Regal—a fine scotch—just what he needed. He threw back four shots immediately, then took the bottle and glass over to the couch and flopped down.

It wasn't going to end this way. He wasn't going to let it.

He didn't care what Irene said. He had a right to at least try to win her back—didn't he? A sound, almost like a sob, escaped him. Didn't he?

Irene's voice echoed in his head. *You've done enough damage to this family.* He *had* done terrible damage to Rose and her father. He had left Rose defiled and pregnant and had left her father a disgraced criminal. He was so ashamed of himself that it was unbearable. Colin took another shot. Joseph West was young and rich, traveled in the same circles as Rose, and obviously loved her. Perhaps Irene was right. Maybe Colin should just stay out of it. He was sure Joseph would be a good father to the child. Colin felt his throat tighten as he thought that. Joseph would be a good father to *Colin's* child. Colin threw back another shot, then leaned back. *Stay out of it. It's all your fault anyway. You deserve every bit of pain you get.* And he felt himself slip into unconsciousness.

Colin's first day at NATO started with a headache that had been with him for two days straight. He had been downing aspirin since waking up yesterday. Ignoring the urge to begin drinking the minute he opened his eyes, he got up, showered, and then went about the business of making the apartment his own, putting away his things and shuffling the contents until he had everything the way he wanted it. He went out to the grocery store and stocked the cabinets and fridge, then cooked himself a light meal—his stomach wasn't ready for much, considering the bender he'd gone on the night before. The one thing he *didn't* do was allow himself to think about anything to do with Rose—at least he *tried* not to think about her, or his child—her child, not his, at least not anymore. Had he stayed around and risked what *she* was willing to risk, then the child would be his. Now, the child would be Joe West's. And maybe it was better that way.

Rose snapped on her bra, then went over to the standing mirror. She turned to the side. Her tummy curved out a bit more than usual, but she wasn't very far along in her pregnancy. Still, it was good she'd be married soon. People were already gossiping about her because of the trial. The last thing she needed was more gossip. Despite this predicament, she stubbornly thought to herself that she wouldn't change a thing about the night she and Colin made love, even if her embarrassment was published on the front page of the New York Times. She would always adore Colin and would never be sorry for the brief time they had together. Joe was a wonderful man, and she was determined to be the best wife to him she could be, but secretly, she was glad that this baby was Colin's. She would always have a little part of the man who had stolen her heart. She rubbed her belly tenderly, imagining holding and caring for the baby.

She wondered what Colin was doing now. Was he in London, or had they sent him to some exotic place? Was he chasing bad guys in Morocco, going undercover in East Germany, or stealing enemy secrets in Russia? Rose hoped he was safe. Did he think about her from time to time? She was sure he had loved her as deeply as she loved him. He had just been afraid to go forward. The scare her father cooked up worked in its own weird way. It was meant to frighten *her*, but it had frightened Colin instead. In the end, the general had succeeded, just as he always did. The famous strategist, except this time, he had paid dearly for it.

Her father had lost his reputation, his hope for his daughter ever to become queen of the White House, and he had lost the respect of his only child. Rose had sent him off to live out his probation on Martha's Vineyard. She could barely stand to look at him. Whether or not she would allow him to have a relationship with his grandchild remained to be seen. He didn't even know she was pregnant. That was *her* secret—a secret she had shared only with Irene and Joe. Joe—what a good man he was. When she told him about the pregnancy, he had offered to marry her.

Joe knew her feelings. She had been candid with him. And with his curly hair and blue eyes, he had similar features to Colin's. It wouldn't be a stretch for people to believe the baby was his. They would just have to pretend it was premature when the time came. That was why this wedding had to happen soon—the sooner, the better.

Of course, Rose had some misgivings about this coupling. Joe had a snobbish streak. Like Rose, he had been wealthy all his life, but unlike Rose, he hadn't learned much compassion for those who weren't equally blessed. From time to time, during their friendship, that had caused a bit of friction between them. When Rose had run charity drives for the homeless, Joe used to scoff at her and say those folks should get jobs. He opposed the Civil Rights bills Rose was so interested in when politics came up during dinner parties. Sometimes, she wished Joe could be poor for just a few weeks so he could see what it was like for people who didn't have the same opportunities as him. Rose remembered stories her mom had shared with her that opened her mind and her heart to those who were less fortunate.

Rose shook herself out of her thoughts and continued dressing. Whatever the case, Joe was compassionate to Rose, and that was most important right now. Quickly downing the egg and toast Irene had made for her, Rose planned out her day. She had to return books to the library, do a fitting for her gown—not a wedding gown exactly, but it was the gown she was going to wear to get married—then she had to pick up the rings she and Joe had decided on. She'd be busy.

Very conscious of the tiny life growing within her, she had a hard time keeping her mind on her errands. Thoughts of

Colin interrupted her wherever she went. How in the world would she go on with her life when she couldn't concentrate on anything but him? There were moments she even thought she spotted him on the street. Maybe she was out of her head. Or perhaps this craziness just came with pregnancy. After she had the baby, would she snap back to normal?

She wished she could have a drink, but that wouldn't be good for the baby. They all said that the placenta would protect the baby from whatever she put in her body, but she didn't believe it. From her perspective, all the junk she ate, drank, and breathed probably went straight to that little helpless thing, and she wanted everything to be as pure as possible. She rubbed her belly again. She might not have been able to nurture her relationship with Colin, but she was going to nurture this little being as best she could. Maybe someday he would know, he would know this child was his, and he'd be glad. Or maybe he'd be sorry he missed it.

She bit her lip. She didn't want to be bitter, but an edge of bitterness crept in. There were moments she wished she could kick Colin in the shins. He had left her right when things were getting tough. He wasn't there when she faced her father's trial, and he wasn't here now. He was a terrible human being. She shook her head slightly when she realized she had been staring into a store window for the last ten minutes, contemplating. Catching her own reflection, she scowled. *You're a fool.*

Turning around, she glanced across the street and met the stare of familiar blue eyes. A passing bus blocked him momentarily, but she instantly knew it was Colin. Cars moved back and forth between them, but they both stood where they were, peering into each other's faces. Almost in synchrony, they moved toward the corner. She began to step off but then waited for him to cross to her. He reached out, then pulled back. Then they both stepped up to the sidewalk.

"Rose, it's wonderful to see you again." He leaned over her. She thought for a moment that she could feel the heat from his body but soon realized it was her own temperature rising. Her heart was pounding, and her cheeks were burning from being so near him.

"Colin," she stammered, "I didn't know you were in town."

"I got here two days ago."

"And you didn't call me?" She felt tears squeeze at her eyes and fought to hold them back.

"I . . . uh . . . actually . . ."

She shook her head. "That's okay. I know you're a busy man." She was embarrassed by the deep swallow that followed her words. How could she swallow? It felt like her throat was closing. Then, the baby jumped in her womb. *Did it have to happen now, that first movement, the first time I felt it?* Rose lifted her hand to her belly.

Colin's eyes dropped to her waist. "Are you okay, Rose?"

"Uh-huh. Fine." She nodded. "Well, it was good running into you. Um, are you going to be around long?"

"A few weeks."

"I see." Rose looked left and right. "Could we . . . could we . . . get together . . . do you think?"

"Would that be okay with Joe?" Colin's smile faltered.

"I'm not married yet." Rose looked up at him with a wide-open gaze. Perhaps he could read the shred of hope there.

Colin met her eyes, then looked down. He glanced back up and said, "I'm staying in a temporary apartment at Tudor City." He gave her the number. "I'd very much like to see you . . . if it's okay with Joe."

She nodded.

"When is the wedding?"

Rose shrugged. "Soon, I guess."

"You guess?"

She swallowed a few times. "Soon, for sure. I guess."

"He seems like a nice man." Colin shifted feet. "Irene likes him."

"Irene?" Rose looked up at him, baffled. "When did you see Irene?"

Colin looked at his watch. "I've got to get going, Rose." He put a hand on her arm, then smiled at her. "It was really good to see you."

Before she could say anything else, he was off down the sidewalk at a pace she could never keep up with. *When did he see Irene?*

Chapter Twenty-Two: His Voice Faded

"Cheers!" Georgia and Teresa raised glasses of champagne and clinked with Rose's glass of white grape juice. "Three days to go, Rose, and then you'll be a wife."

Rose nodded and sipped. The date was chosen, and Rose felt like she was sliding down a ramp—a ramp that was so slippery there was no turning around. Did she want to turn around? She needed this marriage, didn't she? Still, every time she thought about it, her stomach twisted, and she felt a jab that traveled all the way down into her thighs. *This is a mistake.* Images of Colin clouded her mind, she could barely even envision Joe's face when she thought about the future, and she was supposed to be marrying him in less than a week.

"Rose? Rose? Earth to Rose." Georgia poked her. "Are you there?"

Rose shook her head. "Sorry. Daydreaming."

"Thinking about the wedding night?" Teresa grinned at her. "I've got just the thing for that." She shoved a wrapped box at Rose. "Shower gift!"

Rose took the present and began to open it. "Thank you both for making this a celebration. It seems that after the embarrassment of the trial, you're my only friends."

Georgia gave Rose a hug. "We'll always stick by you, Rose. None of this was your fault. Besides, you would've done the same for us."

Rose nodded, then pushed back the top of the box. A filmy

negligee lay under the tissue paper. She lifted it up and chuckled. "Good grief, Teresa, this is barely anything at all."

Teresa laughed. "That's the point. You're such a prude, Rose." She shook her head and gave Rose's arm a push.

Rose wondered what Teresa would think if she knew that Rose was sitting there with a baby in her belly right now—not as much of a prude as Teresa imagined.

Georgia's gift was similar, only in a different color. The girls made a few more wedding night jokes and continued to sip their champagne. They asked Rose if she was scared, and Rose felt guilty about pretending to be a virgin. She didn't say that outright, but she feigned ignorance while all she could think about was that one incredible evening with Colin before those two horrible men came and dragged her away. Georgia and Teresa's questions and laughter felt like little machine gun bullets. Rose was glad when the ersatz shower ended. She was tired, and her mood bordered on miserable.

Replaying her earlier meeting with Colin over and over in her imagination, Rose lay in bed savoring the memory of the slight pout to his lips and the curve of his hips as he stood talking with her. His physicality was magnetic, so suave, one hand casually stuck in his pocket. His eyes seemed to reach into her while at the same time they pulled away. Which was it? Did he want her, or was she just wishing? It was so painful, this hope and this despair wrestling with each other.

Rose lay on the bed, then rolled over and pushed her face into the pillow, groaning. The phone rang. Despite the somewhat late hour, Rose answered it. "Hello?"

"Rose?"

She recognized Colin's accent. "Yes. Colin?"

"Rose. How are you? Am I calling too late?"

"No, not at all." She sat up and crossed her legs under her. Leaning forward, she hugged her pillow into her lap. "I'm glad to hear from you. You're still in the city, right?"

"Yes. I'm still here."

"Good. I'm glad." She made her voice as warm as she possibly could. But don't sound too anxious, she warned herself. Don't sound desperate. Still, she *felt* desperate. She wanted him. She wanted his body wrapped around hers. She wanted his face looking down at her with love. She wanted his life to mingle with hers forever. She wanted that more than anything. But the glint from her new engagement ring caught her eye, making her lose her breath momentarily.

"I was wondering, if it's okay with your fiancé, if you might like to come by my place sometime soon. Maybe in a couple of days."

"I'm getting married in a couple of days." She tried to keep the acid out of her voice.

"Oh." The pause was long. "Congratulations."

Did she hear a little quaver in his voice? "Would you like to come to the ceremony?" she asked him. Again, she fought bitterness. "You might enjoy it."

There was a sigh at the other end. "Rose."

"There won't be many people there. I've lost a lot of friends over the past few months. You'd be very welcome."

"I don't think . . . " His voice trailed off.

"Of course. No commitment. I'll send you an invitation and if you're free, come and join us for the momentous occasion. We wouldn't want you to miss it." This time, she was sure the edge to her voice was exposed.

"Rose, I didn't mean to upset you."

"I'm not upset."

"You *sound* upset."

"That's telephone talking for you. Phones can never convey what a person's really feeling. You have to *see* another person face-to-face to really understand." She had command of her voice again.

"I suppose." He sounded doubtful.

"I'd like to see you, Colin, but we'd have to do it tomorrow night. I don't have much time."

"Tomorrow would be fine. Dinner? At my place?"

"Sure."

They set a time, then bid each other goodnight. Rose fell back on her bed. In some respects, she believed this was almost more torturous than not hearing from him at all. What did this mean? Did he want to restart the relationship? Was he as drawn to her as she was to him? Was he trying to keep away from her but couldn't, or was he just playing with her?

No, Colin wasn't the playing type. Something was going on inside of him, and if he didn't give into it soon, there wouldn't be a chance for him to give into it at all, and she'd lose him forever.

She rolled to her side. Under these circumstances, there was only one thing she could do. No matter how tough everything might turn out.

"I wanted to meet with you face to face, Joe. This is something that couldn't be said over the phone." Rose leaned into him and tried to appear as sincere and caring as possible. She slid the engagement ring off her finger and pressed it into his palm. "I just can't do this. You deserve someone who truly loves you for who you are. You shouldn't be stuck with a cast-off who's marrying you because she's desperate to have a father for her child. It isn't fair to you."

He pushed the ring back toward her. "I'm a grown man, Rose. I know what I want. We've been through this before." He shook his head. "We talked about all of this . . . at length. I love you, and maybe one day you'll come to love me. Either way, we have a lot in common, and we've always had fun together. I think we can make a life for ourselves, a good life."

He forced the ring back into her hand.

Rose shook her head. "Maybe, but I don't want to make my

life with you. Not anymore." Then she set the ring on the table next to him. "It's more than just that."

Joe looked up at her.

"I still love Colin, Joe. Maybe I'll always love Colin. I can't marry you when my heart is with another man."

"What about the baby?"

"I'll just have to deal with that, with the fallout. If I must, I'll be an unwed mother."

Joe's lips turned down. "He'll be a bastard."

"Or she."

"Yes, or she. Everybody will call the child a bastard."

Rose nodded. "I suppose so, but those labels are slowly becoming unimportant, outdated, as more and more women are opting to have their babies out of wedlock."

Joe disagreed. "Not in circles like ours. That child will never be accepted in the right places, Rose. He or she will always be excluded. People won't allow bastards into the fold. Think about what you're doing to this child. They'll talk about it, and about you, behind your backs. They'll snicker and turn their noses up."

"And how about you, Joe? Will you do that?" She gave him a long look.

"I'll never turn my back on you, Rose, but if I *do* marry someone else, you couldn't possibly expect me to have you and your bastard baby to my social events or expect my children to play with your bastard children." He pulled back from her.

Rose started. "My bastard *children*? What? Do you think I'm going to have several children out of wedlock? Do you think this is a habit I'm forming?"

"I didn't mean it like that."

"And you wouldn't invite me to things? You wouldn't stick by my child unless you and I were married?" She could hear her voice rise.

"It's not like it sounds." Joe cringed slightly.

Rose stood up. "It's *exactly* like it sounds." She began to walk away. "Maybe I'm making a better decision than I thought." She shook her head. "I don't want my child growing up and becoming a snob. You're being a snob, Joe, a snob."

"No, Rose, I'm being realistic. I'm realistic enough to give you another chance."

She kept walking.

"Rose," he called after her. "If you change your mind and see things the way they really are, call me. Give your child a chance at a good life."

His voice faded as she walked down his long driveway, got into her car, and drove through the tall gates and out to the street.

CHAPTER TWENTY-THREE: IT'S MY BABY

Rose was right on time when she got to Colin's. He buzzed her in, and she strolled around his living room, taking in the view. "The city looks glorious from up here, Colin, all the lights, the skyline."

Colin nodded, then handed her a drink.

"I'm not drinking alcohol." She pushed the glass away.

"It's just club soda."

"Oh." She took a sip, then came around to the couch. "So, how have you been?"

He sat across from her. "Frazzled. Not particularly happy."

"You? Frazzled?" She raised her eyebrows. "You don't seem like the frazzled type."

He swallowed, then took a breath. Nodding toward her tummy, he asked, "Is that my baby?"

She lowered a hand to her belly. "It's *my* baby."

"Unless you're the mother of Jesus, it generally takes two. And even with her, it took . . . " His voice trailed off.

"Is that why you invited me here . . . to discuss this?"

"Partially."

"So, if it's your baby, maybe you'll want me all of a sudden?" She set her drink on the coffee table, leaned back, and crossed her arms over her chest.

"No." He looked surprised. "It's not like that at all. I always wanted you."

She shook her head. "It sure didn't seem like it. You're the one who left town, left me. And during the toughest times. You didn't even call. You just left, no explanation, no follow-up, not even a decent breakup."

Colin pursed his lips and was quiet for a moment. Then he said, "I didn't think we should get married, not after what happened."

"Why? Were you embarrassed to be with such a mess of a family?"

His eyes widened. "No, of course not. The only thing I cared about was you."

"That makes no sense, Colin. I felt absolutely no care from you whatsoever. You left me stranded." Her voice choked.

"I left you *safe*." His words snapped across the table at her.

"Safe?"

"If you were with me, your life would have been in constant danger. Your father was right about that. I realized the truth after he took you."

"That's ridiculous."

"No, it's not. If you were married to an agent, you'd be vulnerable to any enemy who wanted to retaliate, any who wanted to manipulate. I couldn't put you into that kind of situation. When I came out of the shower and you were gone, I had no idea what happened to you. The thought of—" The words broke off, and he ran a hand through his hair.

"So, you chickened out," she whispered.

Shooting straight up, he came to her side of the living room and towered over her. "I did *not* chicken out. I did the right thing."

"Shouldn't *I* have had a say about our future? After all, as it turned out, our future had a very big impact on *my* life." She rubbed her belly again.

Colin groaned and threw himself down next to her, putting his head in his hands. "I didn't know. I didn't know. And now . . . " He shook himself, then sat up straighter. "But now you've got someone else. Someone to take care of both of you." He didn't meet her eyes as he picked up his drink and took a long gulp.

"Do you still want to know if it's yours?"

He shook his head. "I already know."

"And you'll just give up . . . like that. You'll give up your baby to another man?" She leaned towards him. "You'll give *me* up to another man?"

Colin didn't turn toward her. He just looked straight ahead and didn't answer.

Rose continued. "Can you do whatever it is you'll do next, knowing I'm out there staring into the darkness as I lie next to *him,* wishing it was you?" She took a long breath. "And when I pick up this baby and watch him grow his first tooth, take his first step, will you let some other man share those moments with me—all because you're afraid to lose something you never even bothered to take?"

His breath caught in small inhales, like short, tearless sobs.

"I *need* you, Colin." She reached out and grabbed his arm. "I don't want Joe. I called it off with him, so it's either you or nobody. I have the courage to face the world on my own, but I'd rather use that courage to face the world by your side . . . whatever that may bring. When I was trapped in that room with the blindfold on, I was self-sufficient. I grabbed a gun and shot. I nearly killed my own father. I have great aim, and I know what I want. I want a life with you, and I'm not shooting blindfolded. The trouble with both you and my father is that neither of you wants me to make my own decisions." Her voice broke in frustration. "Colin, why can't you at least hold me?"

He moaned and turned toward her, pulling her into his arms. "I've missed you so much, Rose. I've never felt anything as empty as this." Colin clutched her so tightly that his embrace was almost painful, and his breath was hot on her neck.

She put her arms around him, loving the familiar hardness of his body, the edges of his shoulders, the press of his chest against her, the crunch of his starched shirt, and the scent of his aftershave. All this swirled in her mind as he devoured her, and she began to kiss him. She felt him slowly losing control as he burrowed into her chest. Finally, he lifted his head, and their mouths met. Her heart felt as if it would explode. She wanted to consume him. She had been starving for this.

"I've needed you, Rose," he said, "but I can't bear to lose you. I can't bear the thought of any harm coming to you." He pulled away.

She peered at him, then pushed his shoulders. "I can shoot in a blindfold, Colin." Pressing against him more forcefully, she forced him down onto the couch. His eyes widened as she crawled on top of him. "I can take care of myself. Maybe there'll come a time when you'll need *my* protection. You never know." She raised his arms and held his wrists above his head. A little smirk pushed at Colin's lips as she said, "Do you seriously think I'm going to accept your flimsy little excuses for leaving me a second time, Colin Blake?" Leaning over him, she crushed his mouth with hers. His excitement was obvious as he rose against her. She let go of his arms, and he held her to him. Taking a long breath, she smiled at him. "You're going to marry me, and you're going to take me and this baby wherever you go, because we were made to be together."

"Do I have a choice?" She felt his breath on her face.

"None whatsoever." With a shake of her head, she sealed the deal and then rested her cheek against his.

"Okay." They lay there, Colin stroking her hair, dinner forgotten, wrapped in each other's arms.

End

You May Also Enjoy the Following from eXtasy Books:

The Twisting Time Trilogy
Luann Lewis
November 2021

Twisting Time

During the Cold War, ruthless and cynical British operative David Morse is sent to northern Alaska, where he meets Miri Smith. Supposedly researching arctic water systems, it turns out Miri has a deep secret. One that will twist the couple from 1967 back to 1959 and end up with them held at gunpoint as they try to reach for an unimaginable future.

Facing Fate

When David Morse stepped two hundred years into the future to be with the woman he loved, he entered utopia, but it didn't *feel* like utopia? It wasn't just the pain of going without whiskey and cigarettes. He had to get used to being a father and contend with a future mother-in-law who disliked him. When David's nightmares begin, it becomes obvious that David's fate could change the world.

Defying Destiny

David Morse must travel further into a future where a horrifying discovery awaits. Determined to change the course of fate, he travels to a land where the inhabitants live dangerous lives. David must befriend their dazzling female leader in order to stop the violent plans and save his family.

About the Author

Luann Lewis is a Chicago native who has dabbled in varied genres, having had over two dozen stories, essays, and poems published in print and online. Along with having a piece performed professionally as a podcast, she has authored an educational web series for Newton County, Georgia. Currently, she is working on her *Twisting Time* series of romantic novels.

www.ingramcontent.com/pod-product-compliance
Lightning Source LLC
LaVergne TN
LVHW010110170826
845678LV00012B/2332

* 9 7 8 1 4 8 7 4 4 0 3 2 9 *